BURDENS BENEATH THE HYMNS

THE UNBURDENED SERIES
BOOK ONE

JR GRAY-HEIM

JOSADAH PUBLISHING CO.

Burdens Beneath the Hymns

Copyright © 2025 by JR Gray-Heim

All rights reserved. No part of this publication may be reproduced, distributed, or transmitted in any form or by any means—including photocopying, recording, or other electronic or mechanical methods—without the prior written permission of the author, except in the case of brief quotations embodied in critical reviews and certain other noncommercial uses permitted by copyright law.

Published by **Josadah Publishing Co.**

Raeford, North Carolina

Paperback ISBN: 978-1-7373626-3-0

Hardcover ISBN: 978-1-7373626-8-5

Ebook ISBN: 978-1-7373626-4-7

BEFORE YOU BEGIN

FROM THE AUTHOR

While this story may echo parts of our own journeys, I want to remind you—

your story cannot be confined to the covers of a book.

The pages here may close, but your chapters are still being written, every single day.

The Unburdened Series was born from a deep place of reflection —of faith and fear, of belonging and breaking free. For so many within the LGBTQIA+ community, our stories are threaded with both beauty and ache. They hold the weight of silence, of discovery, of learning to love ourselves in a world that sometimes asks us not to.

If these pages resonated with you—if they stirred something heavy, familiar, or even healing—please know this:

You are not alone.

The path to acceptance, to peace, and to joy is ongoing, and you are worthy of every word yet to be written.

When our stories meet trauma, heartbreak, or isolation, they don't end there.

They evolve.

They bloom through resilience, through love, through chosen family and community.

Below are a few places that exist to listen, to help, and to remind you that your story still matters—

and it always will.

Wherever you are, however your story unfolds—

you are seen.

You are valued.

You are loved.

Thank you for walking through these pages with me.

I am deeply honored to share this journey with you.

— **JR Gray-Heim**

LGBTQIA+ Support & Crisis Resources

The Trevor Project — 24/7 crisis and chat support for
LGBTQIA+ youth
thetrevorproject.org
1-866-488-7386 | Text **START** to 678-678

Trans Lifeline — Peer support and resources by and for trans
people
translifeline.org
1-877-565-8860

GLAAD — Advocacy, awareness, and visibility for LGBTQIA+
lives
glaad.org

The National Alliance on Mental Illness (NAMI) — Mental
health and identity-based support
nami.org/LGBTQ

PFLAG — For LGBTQIA+ individuals, their families, and allies
pflag.org

Dedication

For my Aunt Sharon—
through every season, every trial, you were my rock, my confidante, and
my best friend. I carried your faith in me like a compass, always
striving to make you proud.
I pray heaven has a library, so you can be the first to turn these pages.

CONTENTS

*"Every beginning sounds like silence before the hymn. And then—
someone breathes."*

CHAPTER 1

THE HOLLOW AMEN

Growing up in the South meant two things were certain: summers that clung to your skin like a second layer, and a life stitched together by church. Not just Sundays, but Wednesday nights, weeklong revivals, youth camps, and the steady hum of preachers who seemed to believe fire and brimstone could be hammered into children until they glowed holy.

The Shelton family was no exception. Van's father, Jeff Shelton, once a preacher himself, had decided it was time to find a new church home. In the South, the choice mattered almost as much as where you went to school. It wasn't just faith—it was reputation, belonging, a family's social compass.

Van hated the search. At fourteen, the thought of stepping into new sanctuaries and shaking new hands felt more like punishment than hope. He was slim, his frame still trying to catch up to his age, his short black hair spiked at the front like a half-hearted attempt at confidence. His pewter wire glasses sat slightly crooked on his nose, making him look studious in a way he didn't always feel. He'd just escaped Levi "Husky" jeans, finally wearing hand-me-down name brands scavenged from families with better incomes. His mother, Millie, always found a way to make do. Clothes helped him look the part, but they didn't erase his awkwardness.

That morning, their search brought them to a towering A-frame church. Its stucco walls reached toward the sky, medieval-style doors framed by narrow tinted windows that glinted in the morning sun. Van strained to hold one of the doors open for his mother, only to stumble under its weight until his father's arm reached over his head, swinging it wide with ease. His mother and younger sister, Emmalee, slipped through under his father's arm, leaving Van caught in the door's pull as it slammed shut behind him.

Inside, the vestibule was alive with chatter. Perfume and cologne collided in the air, the sharp tang of Brut mixing with sweet florals until Van's nose twitched. Mauve carpet stretched wall to wall, clashing with brick pillars and etched-glass double doors that led into the sanctuary. Through the panes, he caught glimpses of rows of mauve-upholstered pews. The color was so overwhelming it looked as if someone had spilled Pepto-Bismol and called it holy.

Before Van could recover, Aunt Leslie appeared, turquoise fabric swishing as she approached. Her husband, Uncle David, the oldest in the Shelton family, followed close behind in a pressed gray suit, a burgundy clip pinned to his chest announcing him as DEACON. Leslie swept Van's mother into a hug, her perfume clinging thick as she turned next to Van, enveloping him in the stiff scratch of her over-starched collar. Her feathered Princess Diana haircut bounced with every exaggerated motion.

"You've come on the perfect Sunday," Leslie announced brightly. "Our new pastor's first sermon. And his son is right around your age, Van. I'll make sure you two meet."

The words settled heavy in Van's chest. Another introduction. Another forced smile.

The sanctuary loomed larger than anything he'd known. Cathedral ceilings rose high above, chandeliers dangling like pale giants overhead. A glossy grand piano sat tucked beside the choir loft, its polished surface catching the light. The pews stretched endlessly, room enough for three hundred people—so different from the small congregation Van had grown up in.

A sharp snap of Leslie's fingers jolted him from staring up at the lights. "Pay attention, honey," she said with a knowing smile. "This is important."

It wasn't the sermon she meant. It was a performance.

They followed her into a pew, careful not to trespass on seats already claimed by families across generations. In the shuffle, Van's knees smacked against the wooden back of the pew ahead of him, the sound sharp enough to turn the head of an older woman with silver hair and twinkling eyes.

"Well, bless your heart," she said with a lazy Southern drawl. "They cram us so tight you're bound to leave bruised." She leaned closer, lowering her voice to a conspiratorial whisper. "And wait till she starts singing." The woman tipped her chin toward the back corner, where a towering figure stood draped in a gaudy, jungle-print dress. "Sounds like a wounded cat in Elvis's jungle room."

Her shoulders shook with laughter as she turned back, leaving Van red-faced. His mother's fingers pinched his arm sharply, a warning as clear as words. Behave.

The sanctuary buzzed with conversation as an overly dramatic pianist filled the room with a hymn. Van's father and Uncle David returned, squeezing into the pew and forcing the family into the clumsy dance of standing, sliding, sitting again. Finally, the music minister took the pulpit, his voice booming over the chatter.

The congregation rose in unison.

Van hesitated, caught in his daze, until he realized he was the only one still seated. He scrambled to his feet, careful this time not to bruise his knees. In this church, every motion mattered. Every bow of the head, every lifted voice was part of the display.

Van joined the hymn, his voice low but present. Because here, participation wasn't optional. Here, faith wasn't just belief. It was the appearance.

The sanctuary shifted as the opening hymns began. From the rafters above the choir loft, a projection screen lowered smoothly, covering the tall baptismal. The first words of the morning appeared in block letters, and the music director, sweating under the lights, raised his arms like a conductor calling an orchestra to life.

The congregation rose as one. The sound filled every corner of the mauve-carpeted room, voices layering into something both chaotic and strangely unified. The music was different here —more polished, more eager—than what Van was used to. His old church had been small, their hymns slow, the organ's wheeze often louder than the voices. Here, the tempo quickened. People clapped. The air itself seemed brighter.

Van hesitated, then opened his mouth to sing. He knew some of the songs, or at least enough of the choruses to follow along. The words slid easily off his tongue, carried by the sheer volume of those around him. For a moment, he felt hidden in it, his voice blending into something larger than himself.

Then he remembered what the old woman in front of him had said before service began. Maebelle.

Curious, he leaned slightly to listen—and there it was. Rising above the congregation's harmony came a noise so startling it made Van bite down on the inside of his cheek to stifle a laugh. A cross between a cow in heat and a wail of pain, it poured from the back rows with relentless force. The older woman hadn't exaggerated. If anything, she'd undersold it.

Van dropped his head, pretending to study the lyrics on the screen, but his shoulders shook. His mother's sharp glance landed on him, a warning in silence. He straightened, swallowed, and forced himself into the rhythm again.

The music went on like that—stand, sing, sit. Stand, sing, sit.

By the third round his knee throbbed, still sore from colliding with the pew earlier, but he didn't dare linger in his seat when the rest of the church rose. In this place, participation was everything.

Finally, the last song faded. The music director, wiping his forehead, gestured toward the front pew where a family waited.

"Church," he announced, still breathless from his performance, "today is a day of great joy. We welcome our new pastor, Brother Rich Davis, his wife, Denise, and their children."

Heads turned. Whispers fluttered through the crowd.

The Davis family rose together. They looked as though they'd stepped straight from a catalog—perfect posture, perfect smiles, every detail deliberate. Pastor Rich stood tall, a pressed suit draped neatly across his shoulders, a maroon Bible tucked beneath one arm. His wife, Denise, held herself with practiced poise, her skirt suit immaculate, her wave graceful.

Their daughters stood between them like carefully placed ornaments: Mary, the oldest, taller than the others and already carrying her mother's elegance; and the twins, Ruth Ann and Gwyneth, identical ringlets bouncing as they waved shyly to the congregation.

And then—Jeremiah.

He slipped slightly into the aisle, giving the church a better view. His blond hair caught the chandelier's glow, strands shimmering like sunlight on water. His eyes—clear, unyielding blue—swept across the room. The pressed red-and-white checkered shirt he wore clung to him, tucked neatly into khakis, every crease sharp. Around his neck, a rope necklace rested, a single white shell rising and falling against his tan skin as he breathed.

Van's gaze locked there, unwilling to move. It was as though Jeremiah carried light with him, the kind that made everything else blur at the edges. The sight pressed against something Van didn't yet have words for—both awe and unease.

The congregation applauded warmly. Jeremiah smiled faintly

before turning back toward his family, but the image lingered, carved into Van's mind.

Pastor Rich approached the pulpit. He clipped on a microphone already waiting for him and rested one broad hand on the lectern. His voice filled the room—smooth, steady, touched with just enough Southern drawl to sound familiar but not heavy. He spoke of new beginnings, of gratitude, of God's hand guiding them to this church.

From the pew, Van's aunt Leslie practically glowed, her expression stretched into a grin so wide it looked painted on. She had waited for this day, that much was clear.

When Pastor Rich called for prayer, the congregation bowed. Van lowered his head too, but his eyes stayed open, locked on the cross draped in colored silk behind the choir loft.

A restlessness stirred inside him. The words of the prayer blurred, replaced instead by his father's voice from months ago—sharp, indignant in the grocery store checkout line.

"You know that just ain't right!"

Van had stood there, silent, as his father waved a magazine headline like proof of the world's decay. Ellen DeGeneres smiling under bold letters: YEP, I'M GAY. His father's anger was so loud the cashier had flinched. His mother had kept her head down, busying herself with coupons. Van had stared at the floor, cheeks burning.

That memory pressed into him now, layered against the sight of Jeremiah, golden under the chandelier. The clash was dizzying. Attraction and guilt collided in his chest until he didn't know if he was breathing prayer or blasphemy.

The "Amen" came too soon. The congregation lifted their heads, and the service moved on.

Then came the announcement: teens dismissed for their own service in the new gymnasium.

Van rose, shuffling through the crowded pew in the awkward

sideways dance every churchgoer knew. When he reached the aisle, his mother's voice cut through the hum.

"Don't look lost," she hissed, her eyes sharp. "Follow the group. And remember—what I can't see, God can."

It was both command and warning, the kind of line his family lived by. Van nodded quickly, falling into step with the stream of teens.

But his thoughts weren't on the gymnasium, or the lesson waiting there.

They were on the boy at the front of the sanctuary.

The boy with the golden hair and the eyes that made Van forget the rest of the room.

The boy named Jeremiah.

CHAPTER 2

FIRST IMPRESSIONS

The stream of teenagers funneled out of the sanctuary, their chatter echoing against the glossy brick walls. Van tugged Emmalee along, weaving between church members shaking hands and the smell of lingering perfume that clung to the air like a second skin.

Through a side door behind the grand piano, the group spilled into a maze of narrow hallways. Religious prints dotted the walls—sepia-toned portraits of missionaries, inspirational verses framed in faux-gold trim. Between them, crooked bake sale posters drooped, weighed down by too much glitter and curling scotch tape. The air buzzed with nervous energy, teenagers adjusting their collars or smoothing skirts as they shuffled toward the next phase of the Sunday routine.

The crowd emerged at the back of the church, where a new two-story brick gymnasium loomed in the corner of the parking lot. Its sharp lines and fresh mortar made it look more YMCA than chapel, its fluorescent lights already glowing against the morning sun. Compared to the gothic arches of the main sanctuary, the building seemed out of place—functional, not holy. But this was where the teens belonged, at least for now.

Van hung back as they entered, catching a flash of blond hair through the glass doors. Jeremiah. He was surrounded already—girls orbiting him in a loose circle, their laughter pitched high, their perfume mingling in an eager haze. His presence pulled attention without effort. Even from a distance, Van felt it.

And then the scent hit him—bright, clean, citrusy. Clinique Happy. The cologne of every teen magazine ad, the one worn by boys who seemed untouchable. Van had only ever experienced it from perfume strips in doctor's office magazines, discreetly rubbed on his wrist when no one was looking. Smelling it now, on Jeremiah, made something shift in his chest.

Inside, the gym had been rearranged for "Teen Service." Folding chairs lined up across the basketball court, a makeshift stage pushed against one end. Banners hung from the rafters: *On Fire for God, True Servants of Christ.* A keyboard buzzed faintly in the corner, cables coiled like snakes at its feet.

Adults in polo shirts and plastic name tags welcomed the newcomers, playing matchmaker with quick smiles. They paired visitors with groups of regulars—"Baptist buddies," they called it, though it sounded more like a school project. Van was deposited into a circle of boys near his age, already bonded, their jokes overlapping as if on cue.

They barely noticed him.

Talk bounced between them—hunting stories, football stats, which girls they thought were "smokin'," who could jump high enough to touch the rim. The noise was easy for them, effortless. For Van, it was like listening to a radio tuned just off station, every word clear but meant for someone else.

He sat back, letting their voices wash over him, his eyes wandering. Across the room, Jeremiah leaned casually against the wall, flanked by boys who might as well have been cut from the same cloth—athletic, confident, magnetic. Girls hovered at their elbows, hanging on words Van couldn't hear but imagined were smooth, careless, funny. It looked like a cafeteria back at school:

the jocks' table, transplanted to a basketball court dressed up for Jesus.

Van's own group laughed loudly at some joke he didn't catch. He forced a smile, but inside, his mind replayed the last fifteen minutes. The cologne. The way Jeremiah's hair had caught the chandelier light. The way his presence rearranged a room.

"What's wrong with me?" Van thought. He pressed his hands into his knees, steadying himself. "Why him? Why now?"

One of the adults called the service to order, herding everyone into their seats. Folding chairs screeched against the polished floor as the teens settled. A devotional was promised—something about being a good servant, about making time for God in a busy world. Van braced himself for the familiar cadence, the words he already knew.

He slid into the back row, sinking low. His mind wasn't on the lesson. It was on the pull he couldn't explain, the way Jeremiah's smile had lingered in his head even when he wasn't looking directly at him.

By the time the final prayer was spoken, Van was already planning his exit. He wanted to grab Emmalee, find his mother and father in the main sanctuary, and get out of the shadows of Heritage Baptist before anything else could stir the unease already pressing against his ribs.

True to her word, his mother was easy to find. She was already mid-conversation, signing up for a women's prayer group, her pen scratching her name across a clipboard with sharp efficiency. Van tapped her shoulder, waiting. Her eyes flicked to him, catching the sigh that slipped out before he could stop it. Her warning was immediate: the look. He knew what it meant—he'd pay for that later.

Eventually, his father appeared, peeling his mother away before she could sign the family up to polish pews for the rest of eternity. They moved as a unit toward the front doors, weaving through the throng of church members eager to exchange handshakes and compliments. Uncle David lingered near the entrance, clasping hands like a politician, Deacon badge gleaming under the light.

Van's mother steered them into line to meet the Davis family. The atmosphere shifted, reverent and rehearsed, each introduction delivered with the cadence of a reception line at a wedding.

"Pastor, my name is Amelia Shelton and this is my husband....," she said brightly only to be interrupted by Van's father, interjecting, "Pastor, I'm Jefferey Shelton, and these are our children, Emmalee and Donavan." Van's mother stepping aside of the doorway, locking a handshake with the pastor's wife.

Van extended his hand automatically, a polite smile pasted on. His mother continued before anyone else could. "We came today because David and Leslie told us about your first service. We didn't want to miss it." Her tone swelled with pride. "Maybe we could get our kids together sometime."

"It's a pleasure to meet you and your lovely family Amelia. I'm Denise Davis but feel free to call me Denise." Ms. Denise exuded a level of grace even in the chaos while still beaming a warm smile, in almost relief. "That would be lovely. We're still commuting while we look for a house, but once we're settled, we'd love that." Relief flickered in her eyes at the thought of help managing four children.

Van's stomach sank. He knew better than to protest. His silence was part of the unspoken script.

His mother scribbled their number onto a church bulletin, handing it off like an offering. When the exchange was finished, she stepped away with the same wide smile Aunt Leslie had worn earlier. Her victory was complete.

In the parking lot, she hummed lightly, unlocking the family minivan with a flourish. Van followed, silently praying that her good mood might erase his earlier slip.

He knew it wouldn't.

"Some doors don't open — they swallow."

CHAPTER 3

The hum of fluorescent lights buzzed above the aisles of Kmart like a hive of lazy hornets. Van trailed behind the shopping cart, his sneakers squeaking against the linoleum with each step. His mother steered with the focus of a general leading troops, darting down aisles for toothpaste, bug spray, and a loaf of bread. Emmalee clutched a plastic toy she'd begged for at the entrance, rolling it along the cart handle as though it were a prized pet.

Van's father, meanwhile, had already drifted into the tools section, examining wrenches he'd never buy, whistling off-key like the store was his workshop. The Shelton shopping trips always spread in every direction, Van just another piece of the orbit.

He slipped away while his mother debated between two identical brands of men's socks. It wasn't rebellion, exactly—just a quiet escape. He rounded an end cap stacked with Wrangler jeans and stopped short.

He had wandered into the men's underwear aisle.

Rows of packages stood at attention, lined neatly like soldiers. Glossy models stared out from the plastic, every jawline chiseled, every torso carved like marble. Trunks, briefs, boxer-briefs—different shapes, same perfection.

Van froze, his pulse quickening. It wasn't the first time he'd seen this aisle. He wore the same brand every day, stuffed in a drawer without thought. But this time, his eyes lingered. The men on the packages looked different in each cut—confident, unbothered, bold. Not like him.

Heat climbed his cheeks. Was he just curious? Envious? Or something else he couldn't name? The restless flutter in his stomach felt too familiar—the same feeling that had blindsided him when Jeremiah's smile caught the light in church that morning.

His mother's voice rang from the next aisle, calling his name. Van startled, shoved his hands in his pockets, and hurried back to the cart.

The checkout was the usual chaos: his father joking about Garth Brooks to a tired cashier, his mother digging through her coupon envelope, Emmalee pushing her toy along the conveyor belt like it belonged there. Van bagged groceries in silence—mouse traps next to bread, bug spray against toothpaste—his mind still stuck in that aisle.

The minivan rattled home, a bag of groceries sliding with each turn. His father hummed tunelessly, his mother tapped the steering wheel in time with the Dixie Chicks on the radio, and Emmalee hummed with her doll like a backup singer. Van pressed his forehead to the glass, watching pine trees blur into neat rows of houses. He braced himself. He knew the sigh he'd let slip at church hadn't gone unnoticed. His mother always remembered.

When they pulled into the driveway, unloading began like clockwork: his father grabbed the heavy bags, his mother issued reminders about eggs, Van and Emmalee hauled what they could. Van lingered too long on the porch step. His mother caught him.

"After lunch," she said lightly, but her tone was sharp.

He nodded, cheeks hot, and disappeared to his room as soon as the groceries hit the counter.

The door clicked shut behind him. His room—small, with a twin bed pressed against one wall and a desk stacked with school papers—wrapped around him like the only safe corner in the house. He flopped onto the bed, still in his church clothes, staring at the ceiling fan turning its slow, steady circles.

Jeremiah's face came to mind again—the way the boy's hair had caught the light, how his laugh seemed to fill the sanctuary. Then the memory of the underwear aisle crept in, stirring the same strange, restless energy.

"What's wrong with me?" he whispered into the pillow.

Sleep tugged at him, restless but welcome.

He woke to a quiet presence at the foot of his bed. His mother sat straight-backed, hands folded neatly in her lap, eyes serious.

"Jesus—" Van gasped, catching himself. "You scared me."

Her lips twitched at the slip, but her tone stayed steady. "Van, honey, we need to talk about today."

His stomach sank.

She leaned forward, voice even but edged. "Your father and I have been looking for a place where we belong. Leaving North-Star wasn't easy, but we had to. That church was dying. The old folks wouldn't change. We had to think about you kids."

Van stayed silent, his back pressed against the headboard.

"Today," she said, jabbing a finger into the air, "we found our place. And you—" her gaze sharpened "—showed attitude in front of everyone. That can't happen again."

Van swallowed. "So… we joined?"

Her expression softened just slightly. "Yep. We joined. You must've slept through the vote, which makes your vote a yes." She stood, smoothing her skirt as she headed for the door. "I picked up flyers for the teen events. They're on the kitchen calendar. You're going to be busy—but you'll love it."

Her footsteps faded down the hall, her voice trailing into the kitchen. She always ended conversations that way—walking away mid-sentence, leaving no room for reply.

Van sat frozen. Busy. Involved. Smiling. Belonging.

He exhaled, almost a laugh. She always got the last word.

But under it all, the unease lingered. Jeremiah's grin. The underwear aisle. The sudden weight of this new church life pressed on him like a suit two sizes too small.

The ceiling fan ticked overhead. His mother's clattering in the kitchen drifted faintly through the walls.

And Van lay awake, questions crowding closer than sleep.

CHAPTER 4

NEW RHYTHMS

By the time the Shelton family loaded back into the van for evening service, the sun had already started to dip behind the pine trees. The sky turned the color of bruised peaches—orange and violet bleeding together—and the cold crept in fast as the heat of the day slipped away.

Van pressed his cheek to the window again, staring out at the familiar stretch of highway. The houses grew sparse, replaced by fields patched with brown winter grass and the occasional rusting tractor left like a forgotten monument. His sister, Emmalee, clutched her doll and hummed tunelessly in the seat beside him. His father tapped the steering wheel like a metronome, and his mother sat upright in the passenger seat, posture rigid with purpose.

Church twice in one day. The thought weighed heavy.

When they pulled into Heritage Baptist's lot, the church glowed warm against the darkening sky, its massive A-frame rising sharp and angular, lit from within like a beacon. Cars filled the gravel lot in neat rows, their headlights winking off as families filed toward the doors. Van followed reluctantly, tugged along by his mother's hand at the small of his back.

Inside, the sanctuary buzzed again, though dimmer than the morning's show. The chandeliers glowed softer, the mauve carpet dulled in the lamplight. The air smelled faintly of perfume, starch, and potluck leftovers lingering from the fellowship hall. Families slid into pews with the weary ease of routine.

The Shelton family settled mid-row, Aunt Leslie waving them over from her claimed spot. Van sat between Emmalee and his mother, knees pressed tight against the wooden pew, his eyes fixed on the pulpit.

The choir filed in, smaller than the morning, voices rising in a less polished harmony. The pianist plinked out the opening notes of "Just As I Am," a song Van had heard enough times to know it by heart, even if he mouthed the words instead of singing.

He didn't miss the figure that slipped into the aisle a few rows ahead. Jeremiah Davis.

The boy's blond hair caught the chandelier's light again, that same glint Van had noticed that morning. Jeremiah wore a dark sweater this time, simple, but it clung enough to reveal the lean outline of his frame. He slid into the pew beside his sisters, his posture casual, his arm slung along the back as though he belonged here already.

Van's stomach tightened. He looked down quickly at the hymnal in his lap, fingers tracing the worn spine. But his ears tuned to every sound Jeremiah made—the quiet laugh he shared with one of the twins, the shuffle of his shoes on the floor, the creak of the pew as he leaned back.

The sermon came from Pastor Rich himself, voice booming but smooth, each word rolled out with practiced cadence. He spoke of foundations, of building a life on solid rock instead of shifting sand, weaving metaphors like bricks and mortar.

Van tried to follow, but his thoughts kept drifting. His knee bounced, a rhythm he couldn't quiet. Every now and then, his gaze slid sideways, searching Jeremiah's profile.

And with every glance came the echo of his father's voice in Winn-Dixie, spitting venom about magazines and television. *Not in my house.* The memory clung like smoke.

He shifted in his seat, guilt sparking hot in his chest. What was happening to him? Why him, of all people?

The sermon rolled on, his mother's "Amens" timed like punctuation. Emmalee fidgeted beside him, whispering questions that earned her a sharp pinch from their mother.

When the invitation hymn began, Van felt his throat tighten. Families rose, some drifting forward to the altar, others bowing their heads in fervent prayer. The choir sang louder, voices thick with urgency.

Van stayed frozen. His palms were slick against his knees, his jaw clenched. He couldn't move. Couldn't bow. Couldn't pray. Not with the storm roaring inside him.

Finally, the hymn ended, the lights dimmed slightly, and the service closed in a flurry of handshakes and chatter.

As the congregation filed out, Van trailed behind his family, his chest still heavy. Near the vestibule, Aunt Leslie cornered Ms. Denise again, her voice sweet but loud enough for everyone nearby.

"We are just thrilled to have y'all here," she gushed, gripping Ms. Denise's hand. "Van's about Jeremiah's age—you boys will get along just fine, won't you?"

Van's face burned. Jeremiah turned, catching his eye, and for the briefest second, there was a flicker of something—curiosity, maybe, or recognition. It was gone before Van could name it.

"Sure," Jeremiah said easily, his smile bright but unreadable.

Van forced a nod, his throat too tight for words.

The ride home was quiet. His mother hummed, his father muttered about gas prices, and Emmalee drifted into sleep against her doll. Van sat rigid in the back, watching the world outside slip by in streaks of shadow and light.

The church was their new home. His mother had made that clear.

But Van couldn't shake the feeling that whatever was stirring inside him didn't fit there. Not neatly. Not safely.

And yet, when he closed his eyes, it wasn't the sermon or the songs that lingered.

It was Jeremiah's smile.

Monday morning came with the smell of coffee and frying bacon drifting down the narrow hallway of the Shelton house. The hum of the refrigerator and the creak of floorboards beneath his father's heavy steps set the rhythm of a home already awake.

Van lay staring at the ceiling fan, its blades circling lazy as if mocking his reluctance to start the day. His body still ached from the endless shuffle of pews and standing hymns, but it wasn't the soreness that weighed on him. It was the church itself, that heavy blend of spectacle and scrutiny that clung even now, long after the benediction.

"Donovan!" His mother's voice rang sharp from the kitchen. "Breakfast!"

He groaned, dragging himself from bed. The floor was cold under his feet, the hallway dim as he shuffled past Emmalee's room. She was humming to herself, already dressed for school, her doll propped at the end of the bed as though it needed approval too.

The kitchen table was crowded with plates—biscuits, bacon, eggs slick with too much butter. His father sat in his chair at the head, reading the morning paper as though the headlines had been written just for him to frown at.

"You're moving slow," his mother commented, sliding a plate in front of him. She wore her hair pinned back, apron tied neat. "New church or not, school doesn't wait on daydreamers."

Van nodded faintly, tearing his biscuit apart in silence.

His father lowered the paper, eyes narrowing. "You're not

sulking about yesterday, are you? That was a good service. Solid preaching. A man we can respect."

"Yes, sir," Van mumbled, though his thoughts weren't on Pastor Rich. They were on the way Jeremiah's sweater had clung to his shoulders, the casual way he'd leaned against the pew.

The thought alone made Van shift in his chair, throat tight. He stuffed a bite of biscuit into his mouth just to fill the silence.

Emmalee chattered about school projects, about how she'd promised her teacher she'd bring the Lemon Crumb cake recipe her mother had baked. Their mother smiled, pleased. Their father grunted approval.

Van stayed quiet, his fork dragging patterns into scrambled eggs he wasn't hungry for.

After school, the rhythm of new routines pressed in fast. The kitchen calendar, covered in his mother's looping handwriting, told the story: youth choir Wednesday, Bible study Thursday, visitation Saturday morning. A dizzying schedule.

That night, Van sat on the edge of his bed, staring at the flyer his mother had pinned to the refrigerator and then handed to him again "just so he'd be sure." Bold letters across the top read: *Heritage Baptist Teen Lock-In – This Friday Night!*

He already knew what his mother would say: *You'll go. You'll smile. You'll fit in.*

He leaned back against the wall, notebook open in his lap. He didn't write about church. Not about sermons or hymns. Instead, his pen moved in quiet loops, sketching out the lines of Jeremiah's face as best as memory would allow. The shape of his jaw. The light in his hair. The necklace that had caught against his collar.

And then guilt flooded in, hot and bitter.

He snapped the notebook shut, tossing it onto the nightstand as though it had burned him.

He rolled onto his side, eyes shut tight. But the image stayed, etched sharper than any drawing.

No matter how many verses Pastor Rich preached, no matter how tightly his father's rules wrapped around him, Van couldn't escape it.

Something inside him had shifted.

And he didn't know if it was holy—or dangerous.

CHAPTER 5

FORMS, FEES, AND SECOND THOUGHTS

By midweek, Heritage Baptist had already folded itself into the Shelton household like a new set of rules taped to the refrigerator. The kitchen calendar—already busy with school and bills due—now wore a fringe of church flyers: Youth Choir, Bible Study, Teen Lock-In, Saturday Visitation. Van's mother moved between them with a pen, drawing arrows, adding stars, writing names as if filling a seating chart for God.

"Donovan," she called from the kitchen, "what size shoe are you and how tall are you now?"

He was at the family computer, the AOL sign-on droning its dial-up symphony. "Six feet," he said, not looking up.

Her laugh shot down the hall. "Bless it, son, you're five-six. Maybe five-seven on a prayer." A beat. "Shoe size?"

"Ten," he muttered.

"Good. Dr. Kennedy at eight in the morning. Physical for soccer."

The words hit like a cold splash. Van swiveled in the chair. "For what?"

"Soccer, honey. You heard me." She leaned in the doorway, hands braced on either side, her smile full of decision and not a

25

drop of negotiation. "Jeremiah and the boys signed up for the Baptist league. Your daddy wrote the check. We're in."

A thousand protests crowded his throat. They jostled until all that came out was air. His mother tipped her head, the way she did when she knew an argument wouldn't bloom. "You'll be fine," she said softly, and padded away.

That evening the heat pressed low outside, the kind that made the azaleas droop along Heritage's front walk and made car hoods too hot to touch. Inside, the house hummed with the sounds of dinner—the shush of the oven door, the clink of ice into glasses, the quiet thud of plates set on the table.

Van ate without tasting. In his mind, a clock had started. Physical. Cleats. Practices. Games. He could see himself on a field he didn't know, inside a life he hadn't chosen. His father chewed and flicked through channels after, landing on a game show and frowning at the contestants like they'd offended him personally.

Later, the computer blooped. A private message popped:

SPORTZ4U2NV: Hey man! u ready for soccer?

Van stared at the blinking cursor. He pictured Jeremiah—laughing, easy, already belonging to the team he hadn't even met yet.

TREBLEMAKER16: Yeah. stoked.

The lie tasted small and harmless and necessary.

A new email arrived with a thunk in the inbox. Subject line: **HBC SOCCER – Welcome!** Van hesitantly clicked. Coach Thomas's note was brisk and buoyant: practices Tuesdays and Thursdays at the Recreation center, games on Saturdays, gear list long enough to be a receipt. Water bottle, cleats, shin guards, long socks, ball, towel. Optional: athletic cup.

Van leaned back in the chair. Money turned over in his head

like a slow washer cycle. His parents didn't hide from their arithmetic; bills were counted at the kitchen table where anyone could see. He pictured the cleats, the pads, the long socks. He pictured asking. He pictured his father's face when "optional" came up.

He typed a quick reply, polite and short, then closed out and sat listening to the hollow quiet of the house between commercials.

The next morning smelled like coffee and lemon cleaner. Dr. Kennedy's office was cooled within an inch of frost. Van sat on the exam table, paper gown rustling, while the doctor listened to his chest and said, "Breathe deep," and "Turn your head." There was a form to sign and a stamp to press and then they were done.

On the way home, his mother swung into the strip mall. "We'll just pop in," she said, as if stores were oceans she could wade through without getting wet.

They came out with a sad-eyed pair of clearance cleats (half a size too big, but "you'll grow") and socks thick enough to mop a gym. The shin guards would have to wait. "Your birthday's coming," she said in the car, as if he needed a reminder. "We'll make it work."

That night, Van lay on his bed and stared at the ceiling fan until his eyes watered. He could feel the shape his life was taking, like someone had traced it in chalk while he wasn't looking. Heritage. Soccer. The boys. He turned onto his side and pictured the curve of Jeremiah's smile. Then he rolled back and stared at the ceiling again until it blurred.

He didn't know which feeling to trust: dread of what the field would reveal about him—or the small, stubborn hope that maybe, just maybe, standing on the same grass as Jeremiah would feel like belonging instead of pretending.

Saturday came with heat already crawling up the day. The "Glendover Hills – North" entrance rose like a gate to a different ZIP code—bricked pillars, manicured azaleas, black-shuttered windows peering down at the road like chaperones. The Sheltons' two-tone minivan looked like it had wandered in from a different decade.

Van balanced the jiggling ring of his mother's jello salad on his knees as they crept past house after house. Columns. Porches. Brass lanterns. Mailboxes with gold numbers. He felt like he was touring a museum built for a kind of family they'd never be.

The Davises' place was smaller than the mansions bending the road—a pale-yellow two-story with a wraparound porch, four white rockers lined up like a hymn's refrain. A carved sign over the door read **The Davis Family** in cursive. Beneath it, the verse: *As for me and my house, we will serve the Lord.*

Ms. Denise opened the door in a checked apron, her smile warm enough to fold people into it. "Millie! Come in," she said, and took the sweating mold from Van's numb hands. "Donovan, right?" she asked, eyes bright.

"Yes, ma'am," he said.

"Denise," she corrected gently. From behind, his mother's whisper braided through his ear: "You will call her Ms. Denise." The old dance—proximity and propriety, woven tight.

Inside, the living room was high-ceilinged and clean in the way of homes always ready for company. Fathers had gathered already, big laughs kept at a murmur, as if important people were sleeping in the next room. The kitchen, though, sang with women's voices—the clink of dishes, the percussion of spoons against bowls, the joyfully competitive volume of church friends trying to out-polite one another. It was a good noise. It also made Van's head swim.

"Boys are downstairs," Ms. Denise said, pointing with a potato-salad spoon toward a door by the fridge. "Jeremiah's finishing up. Been working in the yard all morning."

Van slipped through the door and let it fall shut behind him. The noise dulled to a manageable hum. He followed the cool, carpeted stairs to a wide basement room where a brown leather sectional hugged a projector screen like it was regular company.

Seth saw him first. "Well I'll be," he drawled, springing up. "He's really doin' it." He threw an arm around Van and pulled him in, the air filled with the clean punch of deodorant and something that might've been borrowed cologne. The couch shifted as the others made space, their greetings a tangle of elbows and shoulder-knocks.

Colby was all grin and muscle under a snug T-shirt, his energy the kind that made rooms lean toward him. Brandon's laugh came in soft bursts, like he wasn't sure it was allowed to be loud. Two others Van recognized from church waved without getting up, knees bouncing in rhythm like drums warming.

"Where's Jeremiah?" Van asked before he could stop himself.

"In the wash," Seth said, licking salsa from his thumb. "It looked like he wrestled a hog. Hog won."

The basement door at the back cracked open. Van glanced up —and time stuttered. Jeremiah stepped out, fussing his arm through the sleeve of a raglan shirt, hair damp and darker at the edges, the hem of his T-shirt still lifted enough to show a line of stomach, the faint path of hair like a secret pointing down.

"Only hog 'round here is your ex," Jeremiah tossed back, lips crooked. The room erupted. He dropped onto the sectional beside Van with a casualness that knocked against Van's ribs from the inside. Up close, the scent of soap lingered—Old Spice and clean skin and cut grass. The kind of smell that said outdoors and summer and boy.

Van smiled like an idiot and then remembered to stop.

Jeremiah clapped his hands once. "Alright—positions. What do you want to play?" He pointed around the circle. "Colby, you're not a forward."

"Watch me," Colby said, and the bickering began, friendly and hot. Words like *midfield* and *wing* and *keeper* flew overhead like a language Van hadn't been taught.

"What about you, Van?" Jeremiah asked suddenly, torso angled toward him, knee knocking his heat flushed Van's neck. "I —uh—I've never played."

Silence fell. It didn't feel cruel—just brief. Then Jeremiah's voice found it again, easy. "No problem. We'll figure it out. Might put you at the back to start. Get your feet right. You move well?"

Van shrugged, grateful for the mercy of a question without a correct answer. Crossing his legs, and readjusted on the sofa.

"Bathroom's through there if you need it," Jeremiah added, nodding toward a side door as the debate roared back up.

Van slipped away and shut the door behind him. The bathroom was still humid from Jeremiah's shower, the mirror fogged at the edges. The air smelled like cedar and detergent and boy. Van braced his hands on the cool counter and exhaled. He stared at himself until his face blurred into shapes, until he could pretend the person looking back wouldn't betray him by blushing at nothing.

The faucet hissed to life. He splashed his face, patted it dry, waited out a heartbeat that was too loud in small spaces.

When he returned, no decision had been made—only loyalties chosen and then teased. Ms. Denise called them up for food, and the stampede toward the kitchen swallowed the conversation whole.

Upstairs, paper plates flexed under the weight of casseroles and chips. The jello mold quivered, its fruit and secret pecans suspended like trapped fireflies. Van looped the island, found a stretch of counter, and stood there trying to look busy.

A hand landed light on his shoulder. Coach Thomas—tall, tidy, eyes kind in a made-of-granite face. "Happy early birthday, son," he said. "Fifteen's good ground. We'll grow you into it."

Van nodded. "Thank you, sir."

The coach's voice dropped to private. "We're glad you're on the team. Don't worry about where you start. Where you finish is what we'll see." He tipped his head. "And for what it's worth—you've got more people in your corner than you think."

Van didn't have words for that. He didn't trust his face not to show too much. He found a half-smile and used it like a shield.

The boys trickled onto the back deck after they'd eaten, the air warm and the late light laying itself across the yard like folded cloth. Jeremiah hopped onto the porch rail, balanced there, and started telling a story about a camp game that turned into a miracle if you squinted and ignored the broken sprinkler. The others laughed. Van did, too, and it felt almost easy.

When they left, the sun had sunk enough to turn the road home purple at the edges. The minivan's AC wheezed bravely. His mother talked about who'd brought what dish and who'd said what nice thing. His father drummed the steering wheel and said he'd help run drills if the coach wanted.

Van tuned them out and watched the neighborhood recede—porches, columns, lanterns, order. Somewhere in there, under the smell of soap and the thud of boys' jokes, he'd felt it again—the tug toward something he couldn't name and wasn't allowed to chase.

He leaned his head against the window and let the cool glass hold him up.

CHAPTER 6

BOUND BY PRACTICE

Tuesday evening arrived with a heat that clung to the air even after sunset. The City Recreation center's parking lot shimmered with leftover sunlight, the asphalt soft under tires, the white-painted lines fading into gray. Field 3 stretched out behind a chain-link fence, grass cropped short, the goals leaning slightly like tired sentries. A group of boys had already gathered near the bleachers, some juggling balls with casual skill, others tossing their water bottles into the grass.

The Shelton minivan sputtered into a space at the far end. Van stepped out, his new clearance cleats squeaking, the stiff socks itching up his calves. His shin guards shifted awkwardly with every step, too tight in some places, gaping in others. His father clapped him on the back as if sending him off to war. "Show 'em what you got, son," he said. His mother's voice followed: "And don't you dare slouch."

Van swallowed hard and walked toward the group. Jeremiah was already there, a ball balanced at his feet, one hand shading his eyes as he laughed at something Seth said. The sound carried easily over the hum of cicadas, as if the whole field leaned in to hear. Colby was flexing, not on purpose maybe, but his snug shirt made sure everyone saw. Brandon kicked the ball a little too far, chased it, and laughed at himself like it had been the plan all along.

"Alright, gentlemen!" Coach Thomas's voice cut through the chatter, crisp and commanding. He strode across the field with a clipboard in one hand, his whistle already dangling from a cord. His presence carried authority, the kind that made boys straighten without being told. "Welcome to Heritage Baptist Soccer. We're not just here to play—we're here to represent. Discipline, teamwork, faith. That's how we'll win."

The whistle shrilled. "Warm-ups!"

The boys groaned but obeyed, breaking into laps around the field. Van's lungs burned after half a circuit. His cleats thudded on the grass, his arms flailed to find rhythm. By the second lap, sweat stung his eyes, and his chest felt like it was lined with sandpaper. He slowed, falling behind, shame tugging at every step.

Jeremiah jogged back without making a show of it. "Keep your arms lower," he said quietly, falling into stride beside him. "You're fighting yourself." His voice was calm, instructional, not mocking. Van adjusted, dropping his elbows. It helped—barely, but enough to matter. The burn didn't ease, but the humiliation softened under Jeremiah's steady pace.

When the whistle blew again, they collapsed into stretching lines. Colby bragged about his bench press. Seth made a joke about calves that had everyone howling. Van sat quietly, pulling at his hamstrings, trying not to look like he was dying. But inside, something small lit—Jeremiah had noticed, and he hadn't laughed. That counted.

Drills began. Passing. Trapping. Sprints. The ball rolled easily between some, clumsy between others. Van stumbled more than once, the ball ricocheting off his shin instead of his foot. Each mistake felt like a flare, announcing his incompetence. But no one jeered. At worst, a groan. At best, a quick correction.

Finally, scrimmage. Jerseys were handed out—pinnies that

smelled faintly of old sweat, the fabric clinging damp even before the first touch. Van was placed at the back, near the goal. Safe territory. The action swirled mostly at midfield, Colby and Jeremiah darting with speed and confidence, the ball snapping between them like they'd been born with it.

Van planted his feet, heart pounding, every muscle braced. The ball rarely came near, but when it did, he swung wildly, sending it spinning out of bounds. The whistle chirped. "It's alright," Coach Thomas called. "We'll clean it up."

As the sun dropped lower, painting the field in orange streaks, sweat plastered Van's shirt to his back. His lungs burned raw, his legs ached, but he stood. He hadn't quit. That mattered.

Practice ended with a circle at midfield, everyone kneeling on damp grass. Coach spoke of discipline, of honoring God in every effort. Heads bowed. Van stayed low, but his eyes cracked open once. Jeremiah's hair glowed in the last rays, his lips moving in silent prayer, his shoulders steady. Van closed his eyes again, heart thudding.

When the huddle broke, Jeremiah bumped him lightly with his elbow. "Not bad for your first night," he said. Van managed a breathless laugh. "Thanks," he whispered, though he wanted to say more—wanted to hold onto the moment where belonging didn't feel so far away.

On the ride home, his father went on about "running like a sissy" and "needing grit." His mother praised him anyway. Emmalee hummed from the back seat, pretending she hadn't been bored out of her mind. Van stared out the window at the blur of streetlights, every muscle aching.

But somewhere under the soreness, a spark hummed: Jeremiah's voice, steady beside him. *Keep your arms lower. You'll be fine.*

Friday night fell thick and humid, the kind of Southern air that made T-shirts stick before you even reached the door. Heritage's gymnasium glowed with fluorescent light, its wide windows spilling brightness into the parking lot like a beacon for restless teens. Cars lined up bumper to bumper, parents double-parking to drop off laughing kids with overnight bags slung across their shoulders.

Van clutched his own duffel—half-filled with a sleeping bag, a notebook buried at the bottom, and one sad pair of pajamas. His mother fussed at the doorway, smoothing his hair, pulling his shirt straight. "Remember," she whispered, "this is about fellowship. Don't embarrass me." Then she kissed his cheek too loudly, leaving him pink-faced as he hurried inside.

The gym was chaotic—rows of folding chairs shoved aside, pizza boxes stacked high on long tables, soda cans sweating cold onto paper napkins. A band set up on the makeshift stage, cables snaking across the floor. Banners shouted in bold letters: **ON FIRE FOR GOD** and **BE YE HOLY**. The air buzzed with energy —part church, part slumber party, part spectacle.

Colby was already at the snack table, double-fisting slices of pizza like he'd been dared. Seth sprayed soda from his nose when Brandon told a joke, the sound carrying like a trumpet. Jeremiah stood at the center, orbiting friends like planets around a sun, laughing, leaning, pulling people in with every casual gesture. Van lingered at the edge, his duffel heavy at his side, watching the way the group formed and re-formed around him.

A youth leader herded them into a circle. Icebreakers. Games. Trivia about Bible verses. Van's answers came hesitant, mumbled, but nobody singled him out. Jeremiah teased Colby for not knowing the Beatitudes, earning a groan and a playful shove. The laughter felt natural, shared, warm. Van smiled before realizing it.

Later, the band launched into worship. Lights dimmed, hands raised. Voices swelled, some loud and certain, others quiet but desperate. Van mouthed the words, his eyes drifting closed. But every time he tried to focus on the lyrics, Jeremiah's voice rose clear beside him, his hand lifted, his eyes closed. Van's chest tightened, torn between awe and a guilt that gnawed like teeth.

Games followed—relay races, dodgeball, sardines in the darkened hallways. Van stumbled, laughed, even won a round when he surprised Seth in the kitchen, both of them toppling into a pile of folding chairs. For the first time in months, laughter didn't feel forced. It felt real.

Around midnight, the gym quieted. Sleeping bags unrolled across the court, bodies sprawled in clusters, voices hushed but not gone. Van lay near the edge, notebook hidden at the bottom of his bag, listening to the ebb and flow of whispers. Colby bragged about future muscles. Seth spun a wild story about a cow chasing him down a dirt road. Jeremiah chimed in with the occasional sharp punchline, his laugh spilling easy into the dark.

At one point, Jeremiah stretched out near Van, his shoulder brushing close enough to feel the heat through the thin fabric of their sleeves. He whispered something to Colby, their laughter muffled, and Van rolled onto his back, staring at the rafters overhead. His chest ached with something unnamed, something both terrifying and electric.

Sleep came late. When it did, Van dreamed of the soccer field, of grass wet with dew, of running not behind but beside Jeremiah. Of belonging without fear.

When morning light cracked through the high windows, kids stirred like restless birds. Bags zipped. Shoes slapped against the gym floor. Parents honked outside. The lock-in ended as all things did—too loud, too fast, too soon.

Van dragged his bag toward the exit, bleary-eyed but strangely alive. For a night, at least, he'd felt folded into something bigger than himself. Not just the church. Not just the team. Something closer. Something he didn't dare name.

CHAPTER 7

BURDEN OF DAWN

Saturday morning sunlight cut through the Shelton kitchen like a harsh spotlight, slicing across the half-cleared table. Dust floated in the angled beams, visible only when they drifted into the light, like a hundred tiny witnesses lingering over the scene. The table bore its own testimony: two empty coffee mugs with brown rings hardened inside, a spoon sticky with jam, and the newspaper collapsed across the wood in a sprawl that felt careless, almost hostile. The air smelled faintly of yesterday's fried bacon clinging to the curtains, mixing with the bitter bite of coffee grounds still cooling in the filter.

Van sat hunched low in his chair, shoulders rounded, his head tilted toward the soggy cereal that sagged in his bowl. The flakes had lost all structure, swollen and collapsing in the milk until they looked more like paper pulp than food. He hadn't taken more than a bite. His eyelids felt as though sand had been poured inside them, heavy and scratching every time he blinked. The lock-in had run far later than anyone admitted it would, and his body rebelled against the sharp intrusion of morning.

Every sound in the kitchen seemed amplified, as though the night had stripped his defenses thin: the clock's steady tick echoed like a metronome in his head; the scrape of his father's spoon against porcelain grated; the hum of the refrigerator vibrated low, constant, like a warning that never shut off. Even the whisper of his mother's slippers against the linoleum carried weight.

"You look half-dead," his father muttered from behind the fortress of the sports section, not even granting Van a glance. "Don't tell me you stayed up all night giggling with your little friends." His words were casual, but they landed like barbs.

Van's lips parted, but his mother's voice cut through before he could answer. She was at the sink, her apron still tied over the flannel of her pajamas, rinsing out mugs with brisk, sharp movements. The faucet hissed, water beating against ceramic, her shoulders set in that rigid line Van knew meant she was preparing for battle. "It was a church event, Jeff," she said, not looking back at either of them. "The whole point was for him to make friends."

There was an edge to her tone, thin but sharp, the kind of steel she unsheathed when she felt her choices were under attack.

Jeff grunted, rustling the newspaper louder than necessary. "Just saying. He looks like he went ten rounds with Tyson."

The comment hung in the air, mixing with the smell of burnt coffee and dish soap. Van's stomach twisted. He jabbed his spoon into the mush, not eating, just stirring. If he could just disappear into the faded yellow flowers on the vinyl tablecloth, maybe the spotlight would move elsewhere.

He wanted to explain that he had stayed up too late, but not for soda or games. Not even for the goofy contests the youth pastor tried to keep alive past midnight. He had stayed awake for the sound of Jeremiah's laugh echoing in the dark, the way it softened into a whisper when they lay side by side. For the shuffle of movement when Jeremiah shifted closer, close enough that Van could feel the heat radiating in the inches between them.

He had memorized every cadence, every pause, until sleep finally won long after the gym lights clicked off.

But none of that could ever be spoken here. Not across this table. Not with his father's paper shield and his mother's apron armor.

So he mumbled, "It was fine."

His mother finally turned, drying her damp hands on the faded dish towel, eyeing him with suspicion. "Fine? That's all? You need to be grateful, Donovan. Those leaders gave up their whole night for you kids. You should be thankful."

"I am," he said quickly, the words automatic, empty. His gaze sank back into the pale milk and broken flakes.

The conversation ended there, the way most conversations did in this kitchen—his father folding himself deeper into the paper, his mother bustling louder than necessary, clattering dishes into the drying rack as if each plate were a punctuation mark. Van shrank smaller and smaller until it felt safe to slip away without notice.

In his room, the air was cooler, dimmer. The blinds cut the sunlight into narrow strips that reached across the bed. His duffel lay tipped open on the floor, clothes spilling out in a slump, the notebook wedged somewhere at the bottom. He thought about pulling it free, sketching Jeremiah's laugh in broken lines, or tracing the curve of his profile the way the gym lights had cast it. But the guilt came first, heavy and suffocating, pressing against his chest until the thought shriveled.

He flopped onto the bed, staring at the ceiling fan as it spun slow, lazy circles, each blade squeaking faintly when it passed the crooked spot. The sound lulled him, hypnotic, until his body rolled over on its own, burying his face deep into the pillow. The cotton smelled faintly of detergent and the faint musk of his own sweat from the night before.

Sleep dragged him down again, restless and tangled, but

easier than trying to explain the kind of truth that had no place in his father's kitchen.

By Sunday morning, the rhythm of church life returned like clockwork, a routine so well-rehearsed it carried the weight of obligation. The Shelton household moved in choreographed chaos, every room staging its own scene.

From the bathroom, the hiss of his mother's curling iron filled the hallway. "Emmalee, those tights better be on already!" she shouted, her voice bouncing through the house. "And, Jeff—don't forget the tithing envelope this time. It's on the counter!"

His father barked back from the kitchen, "I don't need you hovering—I can manage myself." His shirt hung half-ironed from one hand, coffee mug in the other. He muttered something about "preacher guilt trips" before draining the last of his cup.

Emmalee clattered down the hallway, her patent shoes tapping like castanets. She spun into Van's doorway with her hair bow crooked. "You're gonna get in trouble for not smiling," she sing-songed, sticking out her tongue.

"Go fix your bow," Van muttered, tugging at his stiff collar. The fabric bit into his neck like a leash.

Their mother swooped in a second later, smoothing Emmalee's bow with a brisk tug. "Both of you—enough. We don't have time for sulking or bickering. Donovan—stand up straight. And for heaven's sake, fix your face before we walk into that church."

"I'm fine," Van said, though the words came out flat.

"You don't look fine," his father cut in, carrying his shirt draped over one arm. "You look like you're heading to a funeral."

"Church, Jeff," his mother snapped, thrusting the iron back into his free hand. "Not a funeral. Now finish that shirt before the pastor thinks we can't manage a collar."

The ride to Heritage Baptist was heavy with silence, punctuated only by Emmalee humming "Jesus Loves Me" and swinging her feet against the seat. Halfway there, his mother twisted in her seat to eye Van.

"Smile today. The Davises will be there, and I don't want you sulking. Mrs. Davis notices everything."

Van's jaw tightened. "I said I'm fine."

"You'll be fine when you look fine," she said, fixing her lipstick in the visor mirror.

His father snorted. "The boy doesn't have to paste on a grin like a circus clown. Let him be."

His mother's glare cut sharp enough to silence him.

At Heritage, the sanctuary buzzed with chatter. Aunt Leslie flagged them down with a sharp wave, her bracelets jingling. "Over here! I saved the row," she announced, patting the pew as though she owned it.

"Morning, Leslie," Van's mother said smoothly, sliding in beside her.

"Morning," Aunt Leslie replied, her eyes already sweeping over Van. "Donovan, honey, you look pale. Late night?"

Van's ears warmed. "No, ma'am. I'm fine."

"He's always fine," his father muttered, collapsing into the pew.

The choir filed in, the pianist striking a chord. The hymn rose, voices climbing. Van mouthed the words, barely audible. His gaze drifted—as it always did.

Jeremiah sat three pews up, blond hair catching the chandelier's glow. He leaned toward his sister, whispering, his crooked smile tugging at Van's focus.

Emmalee nudged him. "Why are you staring over there?" she whispered loudly.

"I'm not," Van hissed, snapping his eyes back to the hymnal.

"Shh!" their mother scolded, giving them both a sharp look. "Eyes forward."

The pastor's sermon thundered: *commitment, sacrifice, putting away childish things.*

Van's father nodded along. "That's right," he muttered. "Preach it."

"Amen," his mother chimed in.

Van sat stiff, the words bouncing off him, refusing to sink in.

When the invitation hymn began, he rose mechanically. His lips moved, but his thoughts spiraled elsewhere—Jeremiah's laugh in the dark, the brush of his shoulder. *Could anyone else see it? Could they tell?*

The dismissal came. Families spilled into the vestibule, the morning light harsh through the glass doors.

"Denise!" Van's mother exclaimed, swooping toward Mrs. Davis. "You look radiant. That dress—simply beautiful."

"Thank you, Millie," Denise replied sweetly. "And your children—they look like a family portrait."

Van hung back, edging near the bulletin board. Jeremiah passed with his family, pausing just long enough for his eyes to meet Van's.

"Hey," Jeremiah murmured, barely above a whisper, his lips curling into that easy smile.

Van's chest jolted. "Hey," he whispered back, but it vanished into the crowd noise.

Then his mother's voice rang out, sharp and cheerful: "Van, come here and say goodbye properly."

Heat surged into his face. He ducked quickly, pretending to tie his shoe, heart hammering.

He didn't know if the thrum in his chest was shame—or something dangerously close to hope.

CHAPTER 8

TENSIONS AND SURPRISES

By Wednesday, the new rhythm of Heritage Baptist had already tightened its grip on the Shelton household. Dinner was rushed—mac and cheese scooped onto plates, bacon crumbled across canned green beans, his mother's lemon pie cooling on the counter for later.

"Eat fast," she commanded, sliding into her chair with a notepad at the ready. "Prayer meeting starts at seven sharp, and we're not walking in late."

Van poked at his plate, each bite heavy in his stomach. The thought of another evening surrounded by polished smiles and clapping hands made his shoulders sink.

His father noticed. "Straighten up," he barked. "You look like you're going to a funeral. This is God's house."

Van swallowed the sigh that wanted to escape, replacing it with a small nod. His mother's eyes flicked to him, sharp and watchful. The silent warning was louder than words: *Don't embarrass me.*

The ride to church was quiet, broken only by Emmalee humming tunelessly in the backseat. The minivan's headlights cut through the twilight, bouncing across familiar roads that now led always to the same place: Heritage.

Inside, the sanctuary buzzed differently on Wednesdays. Smaller crowd, dimmer lights, fewer suits and dresses. The choir loft sat empty, the piano covered with its quilted cloth. Folding chairs lined the gym for the youth instead of polished pews.

Van trailed behind his group, half-listening to the devotional about temptation, about guarding your heart. The words blurred together, too familiar, like songs on repeat.

Across the room, Jeremiah leaned back in his chair, arms crossed casually, his attention only half on the speaker. Now and then, he whispered something to Colby, who smirked and elbowed him back. Their laughter was low, conspiratorial—the kind that carried more energy than the lesson itself.

Van's stomach tightened. He wanted to be part of that circle, to lean close enough to catch the joke, to feel the brush of shoulders. Instead, he sat two rows back, pencil scratching half-hearted notes he'd never read again.

When the prayer circle came, teens paired off, some clasping hands, others bowing heads with exaggerated fervor. Van found himself next to Seth, who prayed loudly about "strength against sin" and "being a witness." Van murmured a few words, more to fill the silence than out of conviction.

At the end, Jeremiah brushed past him in the narrow aisle, shoulder grazing him just enough to leave a spark. "See you Saturday," he said casually, blue eyes catching for a heartbeat before moving on.

Saturday. The so-called "parent meeting." Van never understood why they had so many of those. They weren't the ones out on the field running drills. Half the time, all they did was compare casserole recipes and argue about who was bringing snacks. What was the point of all the endless gatherings?

Still, Van found himself nodding quickly, throat tight, palms dampening as though Jeremiah had invited him to something greater than practice—something he couldn't name but felt pulling him all the same.

Saturday dawned hot and heavy, the kind of Southern morning that made the air shimmer before noon. Van expected yard work or errands, maybe the drudgery of another "meeting" where he'd sit silent while adults talked in circles.

Instead, his mother pressed a collared shirt into his hands. "Put this on," she ordered, smoothing her hair in the hallway mirror.

"Why? It's just a parent meeting," Van muttered. "You're not coaching. You're not even playing. Why do you all have to meet so much?"

"Don't dawdle," she snapped. Choosing to ignore Van's moment of frustration displaying a brief moment of disrespect and questioning "You'll see." Van's mother scoffs, with a mischievous look.

The minivan's familiar rattle carried them across town until Van realized where they were headed: the Davis' neighborhood. When they turned into the neat drive with its rocking chairs and Scripture sign, his pulse picked up.

Denise Davis opened the door before they reached the porch. "Surprise!" she cried, and a chorus followed—Jeremiah, Colby, Seth, and a few others shouting in unison. Balloons bobbed from the banister, a banner sagged slightly across the living room arch: *Happy 15th Birthday, Van!*

For a moment he just stood frozen, throat tight. He'd never had a party like this.

"Say thank you," his mother hissed, nudging him forward.

"Th-thank you," Van stammered, cheeks hot.

Denise hugged him warmly. "You're already practically family, sweetheart. Of course we'd celebrate you."

The next hour was a blur of forced productions: cake carried out with candles, group photos snapped, Emmalee tugging at his arm to show off the decorations. His mother hovered close, her smile bright but stiff, correcting him with quiet whispering jabs.

"Sit up."

"Don't shovel."

"Remember your manners—this isn't our house."

Van straightened each time, but laughter from the boys made it harder to keep his edges sharp.

Finally, when the mothers drifted to the kitchen to look at one of the other mother's Tupperware catalog she was trying to sell, Colby clapped his hands. "Alright, enough birthday junk. Basement time!"

The boys whooped, sweeping Van away like a tide. His mother's eyes narrowed as he went, but she didn't stop them.

The basement was cooler, louder—alive with the thud of sneakers and the hiss of soda cans being cracked. Chips and candy spilled across the coffee table, the television frozen mid-video game.

"Truth or dare!" Colby announced, grin wide.

Groans came, but no one resisted. The circle formed fast.

Kyle admitted a crush. Seth howled like a wolf outside until Denise called down in confusion. Colby had to wear oven mitts to untie and tie Kyle's shoes, his hands flapping helplessly while everyone howled.

Then Seth leaned forward, eyes gleaming. "Jeremiah—truth or dare?"

"Dare," Jeremiah said smoothly.

Seth grinned. "Hold hands with Van. Five minutes. No letting go."

The basement erupted with laughter and chants. Jeremiah just shrugged, reaching for Van's hand like it was nothing.

For Van, it was everything. His skin tingled hot where their palms pressed. His laugh came out thin, brittle, but the noise of the group covered him. Jeremiah's hand stayed steady, fingers loose, his grin unbothered.

"You're making him blush," Colby crowed.

Jeremiah shot back, "Maybe he hasn't realized he's my favorite yet. Since you guys are hellbent on acting like your babies!" His eyes flicked toward Van, and in that split second the words seemed meant only for him.

When the five minutes finally passed, Jeremiah released him with a clap on the knee.

But the game wasn't done.

"Van—dare!" Colby barked. "Birthday boy doesn't get a choice."

Groans and laughter rose. Van braced himself.

"Sit in Jeremiah's lap till your next turn."

The boys howled, pounding the carpet. "Do it! Do it!"

Van froze, face burning. But Jeremiah just patted his thigh with a smirk. "C'mon, rules are rules."

Reluctantly, Van lowered himself, the room roaring louder. Jeremiah looped an arm around his waist dramatically, sending the group into hysterics.

Van tried to laugh with them, but his pulse thundered. Every second of contact was unbearable and magnetic all at once.

When his turn came back around, he scrambled off quickly, cheeks blazing, but Jeremiah's grin lingered, almost private.

The game wound down into wrestling matches and soda-fueled arm-wrestling. Van's cheeks hurt from smiling, but inside he buzzed with something hotter, sharper.

Upstairs, his mother's voice drifted down, sharp even under the hum of the vent: "He's acting like he lives here. Forgetting his manners."

The words stung, but couldn't erase the glow that stayed with him—Jeremiah's grin, his steady hand, the warmth of an arm looped around his waist.

That night, staring at the ceiling, Van knew one thing: the field on Sunday wasn't just about soccer. It was about proving he deserved the closeness he'd tasted, proving he belonged.

"To speak aloud is to risk being heard — and to be heard is to be changed."

CHAPTER 9

HEAT ON THE FIELD

The late summer sun had teeth. It gnawed at the back of Van's neck as he trudged onto the rec fields, his sneakers sinking into the baked earth where the chalk lines blurred into pale dust. Heat shimmered above the grass in liquid waves, rising off the ground like a mirage. Even the air felt chewable, thick with humidity that pressed against his skin until every breath was work.

The chain-link fence rattled faintly whenever the sluggish breeze stirred, but the air barely moved. Beyond the fence, the parking lot radiated heat in visible waves, turning vans and trucks into warped, shimmering shapes. Mothers clutched folding chairs, fathers balanced water jugs, siblings darted between cars with dripping popsicles that left neon trails across their hands.

Coach Thomas stood near midfield, a stocky silhouette against the glare. His legs braced apart, whistle dangling from his neck like a sheriff's badge, mirrored sunglasses hiding his eyes. His arms were folded, but his voice cracked sharp as a whip.

"Hustle, gentlemen! If I wanted meandering cows, I'd have signed us up for a petting zoo. Move like you mean it!"

The boys scattered. Colby sprinted out, every step confident, muscles flashing under a sweat-darkened teal shirt that clung to him like armor. Seth jogged theatrically, pretending to wipe his brow as though the sun had picked him out alone. Van trailed behind, heavy-footed, like someone had poured cement into his shoes.

Colby breezed past, slapping Van's shoulder with the sting of a joke. "Pick it up, Shelton! My grandma could outrun you in her church heels!"

The others laughed, not cruelly but together, as if they'd all heard the punchline before. Van forced a weak chuckle, though the words sliced.

Then the ball rolled toward him—fast, too fast. He lunged to trap it, but his foot caught too far forward. The ball skittered past, spinning out of bounds with mocking grace.

Seth's voice carried above the ripple of laughter. "Lord have mercy, Shelton! You're supposed to kick it, not take it out on a date!"

Heat blazed in Van's cheeks hotter than the sun. He jogged after the runaway ball, chest hollow, pretending he didn't hear.

Jeremiah jogged up, smooth as water moving downhill, collected the ball, and nudged it back with steady control. "Don't sweat it, man," he said easily, barely winded. "Everyone trips up the first few weeks."

The encouragement should have helped. Instead, it hollowed Van out more, a reminder of how far behind he was. Jeremiah moved like he belonged, as if the field bent itself for him. Van moved like the ball wanted nothing to do with him.

Coach's whistle shrieked. "Water break!"

The boys collapsed on the sideline, shirts sticking to their backs, water bottles hissing as they were squeezed. Artificial fruit punch powder stained lips and tongues red. Van gulped too quickly, choked, and sputtered water down his chin and onto his shorts.

Seth snorted. "Careful there, Shelton. Drownin' at practice isn't exactly the testimony we're goin' for!"

Colby barked a laugh, leaning back on his elbows, his chest rising and falling with a confident rhythm. He looked carved out of the sport itself. Van pulled his shirt away from his chest, sticky with sweat, wishing he could dissolve.

The second half dragged worse than the first. His lungs clawed for air, his shirt clung heavy, and every stumble felt like a spotlight on his failure.

When practice finally ended, the boys staggered toward the parking lot, parents calling out congratulations, siblings weaving between legs with sticky hands. Jeremiah's father clapped his son's back with glowing pride. "That's my boy. Looked sharp." Jeremiah ducked his head, modest but pleased.

Van's mother waved too brightly. "Great job, honey! You're already looking more athletic. See? I told you this was good for you." Her voice carried loud enough for anyone nearby to hear.

He wanted to shrink into the asphalt.

In the van, sweat drying sticky on his skin, his father turned in the seat, voice sharp. "Son, you've got to toughen up. You play like that, you'll spend the season on the bench. Don't embarrass us."

The words cut deeper than the heat. Van stared at his knees, nodding faintly, shame pressing heavy as stone.

But when he closed his eyes, it wasn't his father's voice that lingered. It was Jeremiah's. *Don't sweat it, man. Everyone trips up.*

And that somehow hurt worse.

CHAPTER 10

THE GUYS' DAY

The Friday night air carried the promise of freedom, heavy with summer heat but buzzing with possibility. Vans from Heritage Baptist pulled into the neon glow of **Galaxy Lanes & Arcade**, headlights flashing against a marquee that boasted cosmic bowling and all-you-can-play wristbands.

The church called it "youth fellowship night." To Van, it felt like stepping into a world where hymns and drills couldn't touch him.

Inside, the smell of nacho cheese and popcorn clung to the air, undercut by the faint tang of rental shoes and floor wax. The lights were low except for neon strips along the lanes, glowing purple and green. Arcade machines lined the walls, their digital bleeps and 8-bit soundtracks competing with the crash of pins.

Colby was the first to explode into the room, arms wide, already shouting. "Boys versus girls! First game's on me if you can beat my score!" He grabbed a neon-orange bowling ball and spun it on his finger before promptly dropping it with a crash that rattled the

rack. The boys roared with laughter.

Seth elbowed Van as they laced up their stiff rental shoes. "Better hope you don't throw

it backwards, Shelton. Don't wanna kill a church grandma tonight."

Van muttered, "Not planning to," but his face flushed anyway.

Jeremiah drifted in behind them, wearing a faded Carolina Hurricanes T-shirt and his

easy grin. He slid onto the bench beside Van, close enough that their knees brushed.

"Ignore him. Bowling's about confidence. Just throw it like you mean it."

Van tried to laugh, though his throat tightened. Easy for Jeremiah to say—he could

probably roll a strike blindfolded.

The games spiraled fast into chaos. Colby whooped with every strike, flexing like he'd

just won the Super Bowl. Seth tried trick shots, launching his ball with two hands

granny-style until it ricocheted into the gutter. Even Emmalee, dragged along with the

younger kids, squealed when she knocked down a single pin.

When Van's turn came, he shuffled to the line, gripping the too-slick ball. The chatter

around him blurred. He swung, released—and the ball curved wildly, clipping just two

pins. Groans rose from the boys.

"Pathetic!" Seth crowed. "My grandma in her church heels could've beat that!"

Before Van could shrink, Jeremiah cupped his hands and shouted, "Nice one, Shelton!

Two more than Seth got in the last frame!" Laughter turned, this time at Seth, and Van

couldn't help the small smile tugging at his lips.

After two games, the group scattered into the arcade. Lights flashed, tokens clinked,

machines howled in mechanical voices. Colby dove into skeeball, declaring himself

"Lord of the Ramp." Seth pestered the girls to race him at air hockey.

Jeremiah tugged Van's wrist, pulling him toward the claw machine. "Help me win one of

these before Seth blows all his tokens."

Van hesitated. "Those things are rigged."

"Not if you've got skill." Jeremiah leaned in, studying the pile of stuffed animals inside

the glass. His shoulder brushed Van's, the citrus of his cologne faint beneath the electric

whine of machines. "What do you think—blue bear or that weird alien thing?"

"The alien," Van said before he could stop himself.

Jeremiah smirked. "Bold choice. Watch and learn."

The claw descended, wobbled, clamped half-heartedly, and dropped the toy inches from

the chute. Jeremiah groaned, laughing at himself. "Alright, maybe you're right. Rigged."

He handed Van the joystick. "Your turn."

Van's palms sweated instantly, but Jeremiah stayed close, his arm brushing Van's as he

guided the claw. The machine lurched, the claw descended— caught the alien by its

head—and, impossibly, carried it all the way to the chute.

The alien dropped with a thunk. Van blinked. "I… won?"

Jeremiah whooped loud enough to turn heads. "Look at that! First try! Shelton's got the magic touch!" He grabbed the toy and shoved it into Van's arms. "It's yours."

Van stared at it, heat rushing to his cheeks. "I can't—"

"Yeah, you can. You earned it."

Page 32Later, when the group collapsed into booths with greasy pizza and pitchers of soda,

Colby raised a slice high. "Alright—truth or dare, arcade edition. My dare? Jeremiah,

you gotta hold Shelton's alien for the rest of the night and call it your girlfriend."

The boys howled with laughter. Jeremiah rolled his eyes but grabbed the plush, holding

it to his chest with mock sincerity. "Fine. But she's way outta my league."

The laughter doubled. Van laughed too, though something in his chest twisted at how

easy Jeremiah made it sound—like even silly dares bent in his favor.

When the night wound down and the vans idled outside, Jeremiah slung the alien back

into Van's arms. "Don't lose her. She's good luck."

Van clutched the toy to his chest on the ride home, the neon still burning in his mind,

Jeremiah's grin louder than the buzz of the arcade.

CHAPTER 11

THE WEIGHT OF EXPECTATION

The Shelton kitchen smelled of bacon grease and instant coffee, the air thick enough to taste. Steam rose from the frying pan and clung to the windows, fogging the corners where sunlight tried to push through. The thin curtains glowed pale gold, tracing stripes of light across the chipped tabletop and the stack of unpaid bills sitting at its edge.

Van sat hunched over his cereal, watching the milk turn gray and heavy. His spoon moved in slow circles, dragging through the soggy flakes like a compass that had lost its direction.

His mother's voice cut through the haze, bright and sharp with purpose.

"Don't forget—youth Bible study tonight after school. Choir practice tomorrow. And Saturday morning is visitation. Write it on the calendar if you can't keep up."

She didn't look up from the skillet, her arm moving in steady rhythm, flipping bacon with a precision born of habit.

"Yes, ma'am," Van mumbled, the words automatic. Each reminder landed like a pebble in a bucket already full to the brim.

His father folded the newspaper down just enough to peer over the rim of his glasses. "And don't start whining about being tired," he said. "You wanted more to do. Said NorthStar was 'dead.' Well, now you've got it."

Van didn't reply. He hadn't wanted this kind of busy—the kind that left no room to breathe. He'd only said it once, that the old church felt stale. But his father had taken it as a challenge, a call to arms. Now every hour of Van's week had been drafted into service: soccer, Bible study, youth choir, visitation.

The house carried a constant hum of doing—always another task, another meeting, another thing that proved their devotion.

BY THE TIME the final bell rang at school, Van felt hollowed out. His friends laughed in clusters by the lockers, voices echoing down the tiled hall. He should've joined them, but the weight of the day pressed him too low.

At soccer practice, Coach Thomas's whistle sliced through the air again and again, the kind of sound that made your shoulders twitch even after it stopped. Sweat ran down Van's back, soaking through his shirt until it clung like damp paper. Seth heckled from across the field, Colby bragged about goals he hadn't scored, and Jeremiah—steady, patient Jeremiah—kept trying to encourage him. Always the same rhythm, the same cycle.

By the time Van walked home, his body ached in small invisible ways. The soles of his shoes thudded against the cracked sidewalk, the heat still rising off the pavement even as dusk settled in. He passed familiar houses where porch lights flicked on one by one, and he wondered if anyone inside those houses ever felt as tired of being "good" as he did.

DINNER WAS a blur of conversation he barely heard. His parents talked about fundraisers, his sister sang nonsense songs between bites, and Van nodded in all the right places, even when his mind was somewhere else—out under the streetlights, maybe, or back at the arcade, where life had briefly felt light.

When he finally made it upstairs, the house was humming with the low whir of the dishwasher and the faint creak of pipes settling for the night. His room waited—half sanctuary, half cell. The ceiling fan stirred the heavy air, its blades catching the shadows like a slow metronome.

He dropped his backpack by the door, then sat on the edge of his bed. The mattress gave a weary sigh, mirroring his own.

His hand found the alien plush tucked under his pillow—half hidden, like a secret he couldn't admit to keeping. The cheap fabric was rough against his palm, but the shape was comforting. He gave it a squeeze and smiled faintly, remembering the arcade's buzzing lights, the clang of tokens, and Jeremiah's grin when the claw finally caught it.

"Shelton's got the magic touch!" Jeremiah had laughed, holding it up like a trophy.

Van had pretended to shrug it off then, but the warmth of that moment had lingered ever since.

A knock startled him, followed by the squeal of hinges. Emmalee burst in, curls bouncing, face full of curiosity.

"What's that?" she asked, eyes wide as she pointed.

"Nothing," Van said quickly, shoving the alien under his arm.

Her grin turned mischievous. "It's a baby toy! Donovan's got a baby toy!"

"Get out!" His voice cracked, sharp and loud, sharper than he meant.

Her expression crumpled, bottom lip trembling. "Fine!" she huffed, stomping once before storming out. The door slammed so hard the walls seemed to shiver.

The silence that followed felt heavier than the noise. Van stared at the door, guilt creeping up from his stomach. He hadn't wanted to yell. He just didn't want her to touch it—to ruin the one small thing that still made him feel connected to something outside this house, outside this expectation.

He pressed the plush to his chest, feeling the shape of it against his ribs. It wasn't just a toy. It was a reminder—a thread that led back to Jeremiah, to laughter that wasn't practiced or planned.

He leaned back against the headboard and stared at the ceiling, the fan's lazy spin catching the dim light. Somewhere below, his mother laughed at something on TV, and his father's low voice answered. The sound rose faintly through the floorboards —distant, but constant.

Van closed his eyes, wishing he could drift past the ceiling, past the noise, past the narrow rules of who he was supposed to be. But the weight of expectation kept him grounded, heavy as stone, reminding him that some things you couldn't pray your way out of.

"Balance is a prayer we whisper while pretending it's control."

CHAPTER 12

COLLISION COURSE

Saturday morning arrived muted, the sky a sheet of pewter over the Carolina suburbs. Clouds hung low and swollen, heavy with rain that wouldn't fall. The air smelled of cut grass and damp metal bleachers, a mixture that clung to Van's clothes as he trudged across the rec center fields. Dew slicked the grass in silver, bending each blade under its own weight. His cleats squelched at every step, his shin guards biting into his calves like cuffs.

His father walked a pace ahead, Styrofoam coffee cup steaming in the cool air. "Remember," he said, not looking over, "don't wait for the ball to come to you. Get in there. Show grit."

Van nodded, though the words rolled heavy in his gut. "Yes, sir."

Beyond the chain-link fence, the field buzzed with pregame chatter—parents staking out chairs, little siblings weaving between coolers, the faint smell of sausage biscuits from a concession cart. Coach Thomas stood at midfield, whistle hanging like judgment from his neck. He barked names, dividing the boys into sides with sharp gestures.

The scrimmage started fast, the opposing team larger, sharper, louder. Jeremiah glided across the field as if born to it, Colby barked orders like a drill sergeant, and Seth barreled into anyone within reach. Van felt himself lagging a half-step behind, chasing shadows he couldn't catch.

His lungs burned. His ribs ached. His jersey clung to his back with sweat that smelled faintly of cut weeds. Every time he glanced toward the sidelines, his father's arms were crossed, coffee cooling in his grip, jaw tight with expectation.

Then the loose ball came spinning toward midfield. His father's voice echoed in his head: *Don't stand around—get in there.*

Van lunged. Feet tangled. A body slammed his shoulder. The ground came up hard, chest-first into wet grass. The world jarred sideways, a whistle shrieked like metal scraping glass. For a moment, he couldn't breathe—just a wheeze, a clawing for air.

"Van!" Jeremiah's voice cracked across the field. He was there instantly, crouched low, hand hovering near Van's chest but not touching. "You okay?"

Van gasped, air rushing back into his lungs like water. "I—I think so."

Coach Thomas waved it off from midfield. "Knocked the wind out. He's fine."

But Jeremiah's eyes stayed locked on him, worry bright and unhidden. Van's chest hurt for reasons that had nothing to do with the fall.

Colby and Jeremiah each grabbed an arm, hauling him upright. The parents on the sidelines clapped, some out of sympathy, some out of reflex. His mother's voice rose clear above them all: "That's my boy!"

Van wanted to disappear into the grass.

THE SCRIMMAGE ENDED 4–1. Jeremiah scored their only goal. The sky still hadn't opened up, but the air was thicker now, the smell of rain stronger. Van trudged off the field, his ribs tender under his shirt, shame heavier than any bruise. His father muttered something about toughness on the walk to the car. His mother scribbled notes in her planner about the Davis team dinner, already planning the next obligation.

Inside the house, the familiar smell of laundry and Pine-Sol mixed with bacon grease from that morning. The hallway was dim, the afternoon light falling in pale squares through the blinds.

Emmalee skipped past, curls bouncing, clutching the alien plush to her chest like a prize.

"Give it back!" Van barked, reaching for it before he thought.

She squealed, spinning out of reach. "It's mine now! Jeremiah's girlfriend is mine!"

The words hit like a slap, sharp and small but deep. "I mean it, Emmalee—give it back!"

His mother appeared in the doorway, hair pinned up, laughing softly. "Oh, let her play with it, Donovan. Don't be so serious."

Van's hands clenched at his sides. He could feel the bruises on his ribs blooming deeper, an ache that had nothing to do with soccer anymore. Emmalee dashed away, the alien bouncing in her grip, blissfully unaware of how much it meant.

Van stood frozen, throat tight, eyes fixed on the empty space where the plush had been. It wasn't just a toy. It was the one secret thread of connection, the one thing he hadn't yet lost to duty or performance.

And now, even that seemed to be slipping from his grasp.

He turned toward his room, the floor creaking under his weight. Upstairs, the fan would be spinning, the air would be heavy, and the window would look out at the same gray sky. But the hollow in his chest would be deeper than before.

Somewhere across town, Jeremiah might be laughing with his

brothers, scrolling his phone, eating cereal without thinking about anything at all. The thought made Van's ribs ache in a new way.

CHAPTER 13

RUNNING BETWEEN WORLDS

Monday evening sagged under a bruised Carolina sky, the heat of the day loosening into a faint, welcome cool. Floodlights cracked on one by one, buzzing faintly as they spilled hard white light across the grass. Shadows flattened; moths turned frantic around the poles, a halo of wings beating against the glow.

Van stood at the edge of field three, shin guards cinched too tight, jersey damp against his back. His ribs still throbbed from Saturday's collision—a dull, private ache he'd learned to hide. Injuries weren't excuses in the Shelton house.

Coach Thomas's whistle split the evening air. "Alright, boys, line it up!"

The team shuffled forward, cleats clattering, laughter bouncing between them like ricocheting marbles. Colby smacked Seth across the head with a water bottle, earning a muffled curse. Jeremiah slid into place beside Van, his grin easy and wordless. Van tried to return it, though his stomach knotted tight.

Drills snapped out in sharp succession: cones zigzagging across the grass, passing lines cracking with barks of "Here!" and

"Switch!" The field thudded under pounding cleats. Sweat slicked faces, the night vibrating with the rhythm of work.

Van stumbled almost immediately—his touches sloppy, his timing late, his lungs hitching. He could feel eyes on him: Coach's, his teammates', maybe even Jeremiah's. His father's voice thudded like a drumbeat: *Nobody remembers the boy who falls.*

Sprints came next. Jeremiah ate up the field with long, effortless strides, Colby barreled forward with raw power, even Seth managed to outrun him by five yards. Van dragged in last, chest screaming.

Coach's whistle shrieked. "Shelton! You run like you're chasing your mama's cornbread, not a ball. Push harder!"

The boys laughed—not cruel but not gentle either. Van forced a crooked smile, humiliation burning hotter than the ache in his lungs.

As they jogged back to the line, Jeremiah slowed to match Van's dragging pace. "Don't let him get in your head," he muttered. "You're fine. Just takes time."

Van glanced sideways, startled by the softness. "Easy for you to say. You make it look... effortless."

Jeremiah shrugged, swiping sweat from his brow. "Been playing since I could walk. You'll get there." He nudged Van's shoulder, just enough to steady him. "Rule number one? Don't quit."

The whistle blew again, snapping them forward.

By the end, Van's legs felt like sandbags, his shirt plastered to his skin. Above them the sky deepened to indigo, streaks of orange bleeding out behind the treeline. Parents clustered at the edge of the field, arms crossed, coffee cups steaming.

Coach clapped his hands. "Good work, boys. Hydrate, sleep, and eat like you mean it. Tuesday and Thursday, same time."

The group scattered—some collapsing on the grass, others sprinting to cars. Jeremiah lingered, fiddling with his water bottle, then tilted his head. "Hey. You did better than Saturday. Seriously."

Van huffed a laugh, pushing sweat up his glasses. "That's a low bar."

"Still counts." Jeremiah's grin was warm, easy, like sunlight cutting through clouds. "You free after this? Mom brought snacks. Sit on the bleachers for a bit?"

The words landed like a stone in water, rippling outward. Small, ordinary—but they felt like an invitation to something larger.

Van swallowed hard and nodded. "Yeah. I'm free."

They sat side by side on the cool metal bleachers. The world around them hummed with crickets, the buzz of lights, the faint chatter of parents waiting. Jeremiah tore open a bag of Doritos, handed it over without a word. Van took a handful, cheese dust staining his fingers. For once, he didn't care if his mother would scold him later for junk food before supper.

As Van chewed, he noticed something dangling from Jeremiah's backpack strap—catching the floodlight glow. A ridiculous green alien plush, stitched grin wide, black plastic eyes far too big for its head. Jeremiah caught his glance, smirked, and unhooked it.

"Don't tell me you've never had a mascot before," he teased, tossing it into Van's lap. The plush landed with a soft plop, its grin staring straight up.

Van fumbled, laughing nervously. "Pretty sure mascots are supposed to be… fierce."

Jeremiah leaned back, pretending to consider. "Oh, she's fierce. Don't let that smile fool you—she'll eat your soul if you blow too many passes."

Van shook his head but kept holding it, thumb running over its cheap felt. The eyes glared like they knew a secret.

The boys shouted from the field, calling for Jeremiah to hurry, but Van tucked the alien against his side, his grin coming easier this time.

They didn't talk much after that. They didn't need to. Their shoulders brushed now and then, and Van's chest felt both lighter and tighter at once. Jeremiah laughed at something on his phone, tilting his head back so the light caught in his hair, and Van thought: *maybe this is what breathing feels like.*

CHAPTER 14

SCRIMMAGE

Tuesday evening clung heavy and damp, the kind of late-summer heat that wrapped itself around skin and refused to let go. The City Rec Center fields shimmered under the fading sun, grass already worn thin where drills had been run into the dirt. Mosquitoes drifted in slow spirals, drawn to the sweat already forming on the boys' necks.

Coach Thomas arrived like a storm cloud, whistle dangling, clipboard tucked tight, his voice booming before he even hit the grass. "Alright, fellas! Tonight we scrimmage. I want effort, not excuses. If you're breathing, you're moving. If you're moving, you're learning."

The boys roared like he'd just announced the state finals. Colby bounced on his toes like a prizefighter, cracking his knuckles with exaggerated menace. Seth, grinning too wide, yanked his shirt over his head to claim a spot on "skins." Jeremiah stretched with quiet precision, movements fluid, blond hair catching the dying sunlight like spun gold.

Van tugged at his cleats, heart drumming a rhythm that had nothing to do with exercise. He hadn't played a real game since PE kickball in middle school. And now—under the scrutiny of teammates, Coach, and his father standing stiff-armed at the sideline—he was supposed to prove he belonged.

Teams split quick—shirts versus skins. Fate dropped Jeremiah opposite Van. From midfield, Jeremiah crossed his arms, grinning like he'd already won.

The whistle shrieked.

Chaos erupted instantly. Cleats tore at the field, voices tangled in a mess of shouts—"Pass!" "Here!" "Mine!" The ball zipped across the grass with reckless speed. Colby barked orders like he'd been sworn in as captain, Seth bulldozed through bodies, and Jeremiah—always Jeremiah—moved like the game bent itself to him. Each touch was clean. Each step cut sharper than the last.

When the ball rolled Van's way, panic flared. His foot trapped it clumsily; for half a second, he thought he might actually manage. Then Jeremiah swooped in with the grace of someone who'd done it a thousand times, stealing it clean and sprinting past without breaking stride.

"Thanks, Shelton!" Jeremiah called, flashing a grin.

The others laughed, the kind that made Van's ears go hot. He forced a crooked smile, jogging back into place, swallowing the stone in his throat. *Shake it off. Just shake it off.*

The scrimmage stretched into twilight. Floodlights flickered awake one by one, buzzing faintly as moths hurled themselves against the glow. Sweat stung Van's eyes, his lungs clawing for air with every sprint. But somewhere between botched touches and near disasters, something shifted.

A clean pass slid off his foot—straight to Colby, who actually scored. The cheer that followed stunned Van so hard he almost forgot to celebrate.

"See? He's learning!" Jeremiah shouted, clapping his hands.

The words landed heavier than the cheers. Van stumbled into a grin, chest buzzing with something dangerously close to pride.

When the final whistle blew, the boys collapsed onto the grass in a ragged circle, jerseys clinging, breaths ragged. The night hummed with cicadas, the air sweet with cut grass and faint charcoal drifting from the neighborhood nearby. Fireflies winked at the edges of the field like tiny spectators.

Jeremiah dropped beside Van, stretching out with arms folded behind his head. His shoulder brushed Van's, casual and electric. "Not bad for your first scrimmage."

"Not good either," Van muttered, shredding grass between his fingers.

Jeremiah smirked, eyes still fixed on the darkening sky. "Better than sitting on the sidelines wishing you'd tried."

Van's chest tightened at the ease in his voice, the way it folded effort into belonging. Before he could answer, Seth piped up, his voice cutting through the circle.

"Hey, Shelton—where's your lucky alien? Thought you'd need her to score."

The boys chuckled. Colby piled on, pointing with his water bottle. "Yeah, bring your arcade girlfriend next time. Maybe she'll bail you out."

Laughter flared louder, bouncing across the grass. Van's face burned hot, words tangling in his throat. He wanted to say it wasn't even his anymore, that it was stupid, that they didn't get it —but nothing came out.

Then Jeremiah's voice slid in, smooth and easy. "Don't mock the mascot. She's the only one who likes you clowns."

The circle erupted again, but this time the laughter bent away from Van instead of toward him. He caught Jeremiah's grin out of the corner of his eye—small, private, meant only for him.

The alien plush wasn't just a joke. It was a thread, invisible to the others but knotted tight between them.

And in that moment, lying breathless on the grass with laughter spilling across the night, Van let himself breathe like maybe—just maybe—he belonged.

CHAPTER 15

THE FIRST GAME

The morning air cut clean through the lingering warmth of summer, sharp with the first whisper of autumn. Van's breath clouded faintly as he stepped out of the van, the door groaning closed behind him. Dew slicked the city recreation fields, turning every blade of grass into a thread of glass. The world shimmered—too bright, too open.

Parents and siblings streamed across the gravel lot, folding chairs bumping against hips, thermoses steaming like miniature chimneys. The smell of coffee, fresh-cut grass, and concession-stand hot dogs tangled together into something that felt half-celebration, half-performance.

Van's mother adjusted the strap of her oversized tote bag, scanning the crowd with the wary precision of someone taking attendance in church.

"Remember," she whispered, low but sharp. "Smile if someone talks to you. Be polite. No sulking."

"Yes, ma'am," Van murmured, tugging at the hem of his jersey. The maroon fabric hung too loose, number 12 rippling when the breeze caught it. It felt less like a uniform and more like a borrowed skin.

Emmalee skipped ahead, her doll waving like royalty from under one arm. Their father trailed behind with the family cooler, nodding to other dads in that brisk, knowing way men did when they were trying to look like they'd always belonged here. But Van knew better. None of them had. This—like everything lately—was new ground.

ON THE SIDELINE, the boys clustered in mismatched jerseys that gleamed wetly under the morning light. Colby stretched with theatrical groans, flexing muscles just to remind everyone he had them. Seth cracked jokes loud enough to draw frowns from parents trying to bow their heads in a pre-game prayer. Brandon bobbed his head to a beat no one else could hear through his headphones.

And Jeremiah—

He stood slightly apart, ball at his feet, tapping it in steady rhythm. His head was bent, jaw set, the morning sun tracing gold through his hair. When he finally looked up and caught Van's eye, a grin spread across his face—easy, confident, like he was letting Van in on a secret.

Van's stomach turned a slow, nervous flip.

"ALRIGHT, BOYS, CIRCLE UP!" Coach Thomas's voice carried across the field, slicing through chatter. He looked born to this moment —ball cap low, whistle gleaming, muscles tight under a faded polo. Clipboard tucked beneath his arm like a weapon he didn't need to draw.

"This is the first step of the season," he said, voice steady but charged. "I don't care if you win by ten or lose by twenty. I care that you play like a team. Eyes up. Hustle. Respect the game. Respect each other."

The boys nodded, some solemn, some pretending. Colby

smirked. Seth yawned. Van kept his gaze fixed on the grass, as if the pattern of dew could give him courage.

Coach clapped once, sharp enough to startle a nearby bird. "Positions. Jeremiah—forward. Colby—midfield. Seth—defense. Brandon—keeper. Donovan—"

Van's shoulders tensed.

"Rotate between mid and defense today. Watch, learn, stay sharp. Your time will come."

"Yes, sir," he said, the words smaller than he meant.

Jeremiah leaned close enough for Van to feel his breath. "You'll be fine," he whispered. "Just play. Don't think so much."

Van nodded, trying to believe him.

THE WHISTLE BLEW—

—and the world burst open.

Blue jerseys surged across the field, voices crashing together in a storm of shouts. Brandon dove early for a save, rolling into the net with the ball clutched tight. Both sets of parents erupted, cheers and groans blending into white noise.

Van sprinted the sideline, lungs raw already. Each sound sharpened—the thud of the ball, the squeak of cleats in wet grass, the chorus of shouted advice from the bleachers.

"Stay on him!"

"Kick it wide!"

"Run, run!"

And then, over them all—his father's voice, unmistakable.

"Get in there, Donovan! Stop watching!"

The words hit like a whipcrack. Heat flooded his chest. He dove toward the play, nearly colliding with Seth. The ball skipped free, and Jeremiah appeared out of nowhere, cutting through defenders with effortless precision. His hair caught the light; his body moved like rhythm itself. He fired a shot toward goal—blocked, but close enough to draw a collective gasp.

Van grinned before he could stop himself.

Minutes blurred into muscle and breath. Sweat stung his eyes, his calves screamed, but somewhere in the chaos, he started to find a pulse—a rhythm that made sense. He learned to read Jeremiah's movements, to anticipate Colby's bluster, to slide where space opened. When a shot ricocheted off his shin and landed clean at Colby's feet, he hardly realized what he'd done until the sideline erupted.

"Nice, Van!" Jeremiah shouted, flashing a thumbs-up before sprinting ahead.

The praise struck deeper than any victory. It glowed under his skin.

By halftime, the score was tied. The boys collapsed on the grass, gulping water as if it might save them. Parents bustled like nurses at triage, handing out orange slices and paper towels. Voices overlapped—encouragement, critique, gossip.

Van sat cross-legged, breath heaving, as Jeremiah dropped beside him. Their shoulders brushed—barely—but the contact pulsed through Van's tired body like a live wire.

"You're doing good," Jeremiah said, offering half an orange slice. "Told you you'd get it."

Van took it, eyes fixed on the grass. "Thanks." The word felt small, almost fragile.

Jeremiah grinned, sunlight breaking through the clouds just long enough to flash across his face. Juice ran down his chin, and Van wanted to laugh but didn't.

The second half hit harder. Legs heavy. Air thicker. The field stretched endlessly in both directions. The blue team pressed harder, voices sharper, collisions louder. Parents' cheers blurred into one relentless wall of sound.

Then it happened—a perfect sequence, brief but brilliant. Colby to Jeremiah. Jeremiah weaving through two defenders like water slipping between stones. A plant. A strike. The ball sailed, spinning gold in the sun, and slammed into the back of the net.

The field exploded. Players shouted, parents leapt to their feet, Seth nearly tackled Jeremiah in celebration.

From the sideline, Van's father bellowed, "That's how it's done!"—like Jeremiah were his own son.

Van clapped, cheered with the others, tried to let the joy fill him. But pride tangled with something else—something sharp and wordless. Because Jeremiah always made it look easy. And Van knew nothing about this ever was.

WHEN THE FINAL WHISTLE BLEW, they'd won—one goal was enough.

The boys crowded together, jerseys soaked, arms thrown around shoulders, laughter spilling into the cooling air. Phones snapped, parents shouted praise. Coach Thomas clapped each boy on the back like he was knighting them one by one.

Van stood in the center of it all, dizzy from exhaustion and light. Jeremiah's arm looped over his shoulders, tugging him into the circle. The sound of victory swelled around them, bright and brief as summer lightning.

For once, Van didn't feel like the outsider hovering at the edge.

For once, he let himself belong.

CHAPTER 16

VICTORY LAPS

The parking lot looked less like the end of a small-town soccer game and more like a county fair that hadn't gotten the memo to go home. Trunks popped open in a chorus; folding chairs shrieked as they unfolded and then collapsed again; the air swirled with popcorn salt, cut grass, and tailpipe fumes. Kids draped themselves across warm hoods, jerseys still damp, soaking up the kind of glory that only a Saturday win can mint.

The sun slid low, painting the sky in dilute pinks and bruised purples. Floodlights lingered over the thinning fields, a high electric buzz, moths throwing themselves at the glow like tiny, devout pilgrims. Parents grouped in clumps: some re-refereeing the game with exaggerated gravitas, others trading casserole alchemy as though it mattered as much as the scoreboard.

Coach Thomas held court by the concession stand, encircled by dads replaying every pass in blockbuster detail. His laugh—big and sure of itself—rolled over the hum of voices. Van's mother orbited the mom-circle, a casserole dish wedged in the crook of her arm, nodding in all the right places while slipping in phrases like "team bonding nights" and "keeping our boys on the right track."

Van lingered by the family van, water bottle clutched like a permission slip. He braced for curfew, for a homework reminder, for the gentle leash.

Seth vaulted onto his dad's tailgate and cupped his hands. "Sonic! Half-price slushies till eight!"

Van waited for the no.

His mother waved him off with a distracted smile. "Go on, honey! Back by ten. And behave."

Behave—always the tag. Still, the yes tasted sweet. The knot in his chest loosened as he let the tide pull him toward Brandon's dented sedan, laughter and basslines sweeping him along.

Sonic was pandemonium. Cars crammed into stalls, headlights winking, windows down as teenagers traded shouts across rows. Carhops weaved between chrome and elbows, balancing chili dogs and neon slushies while dodging some maniac's rogue soccer ball.

The Heritage boys arrived in a ragged caravan. Brandon's sedan rattled like it might shake itself into parts. Colby hung out the passenger window, yelling directions as if he were shepherding a parade. From the backseat, Seth heckled a knot of rival-team girls posted in the corner stall. The girls rolled their eyes but didn't exactly look away.

Jeremiah's family van was already crooked under the buzzing sign. He slid out still in jersey, damp hair catching the pink-blue neon. He spotted Van in the chaos.

"Van!" The single syllable cut through everything—easy, confident, as if it were the most obvious thing to call him in.

They claimed a corner stall like kings. Trays landed heavy— chili cheese tots, corndogs, slushies in radioactive colors. Grease and sugar braided into the air until it felt like you could chew it. Colby stacked onion rings into towers and goaded Seth into one-bite dares; the resulting choking fit brought the kind of laughter that makes strangers grin.

Jeremiah leaned against the van's hood, straw between his teeth, gaze skimming the lot like he'd personally arranged it. When Van drifted close, Jeremiah shifted without thinking, carving out easy space.

"You were solid out there," he said, voice almost lost under Brandon's subwoofer.

Van laughed too quickly. "Pretty sure I just ran around and prayed the ball didn't hit my face."

Jeremiah bumped his shoulder—light, steadying. "Half the game is running. The other half is pretending it was the plan."

The touch stayed. The heat in Van's chest didn't blame the chili.

Chaos bloomed in pockets: Brandon baptizing his lap with a full slushie; Colby fumbling a flirt so badly the carhop broke character and cackled; Seth delivering an operatic rendition of Coach's "Respect the game!"—spit, stance, and sermon.

Neon buzzed above them, painting everyone in electric cotton candy. Van kept stealing glances when he thought no one was looking—the tilt of Jeremiah's laugh, the loose geometry of his arms on the hood, how everything about him seemed unstudied and, somehow, inevitable. Each glance pressed against Van's ribs: awe stitched to ache.

At one point Colby caught him. "You good, Shelton?" he grinned.

Van shoved a fry into his mouth, words turning to salt and starch. The circle laughed—not mean, not kind, just loud. Jeremiah smirked and let it pass like he'd batted a wasp away.

Eventually horns flashed—parental curfew by headlight. Groans rippled. Goodbyes stretched into "one more"—one more joke, one more shove, one more plan that wasn't a plan.

Jeremiah flicked his empty cup into the trash, the arc casual and perfect, then looked back. "Ride with us next time," he said, like he was noting the weather. "More fun than playing chauffeur for your parents."

Van nodded too fast. "Yeah. Sure."

A golden ticket disguised as a toss-off. His heart took the hint anyway.

On the drive home, the Shelton minivan felt shrunken, air thick with post-game analysis. His father broke down plays with sideline authority; his mother praised the Davis family's "great energy"; Emmalee hummed to her doll. Van tipped his forehead to the glass and watched Sonic's neon dissolve into night.

Ride with us next time.

A nothing line. And yet it glowed longer than the sign.

CHAPTER 17

CRACKS IN THE GAME

The second game arrived before Van had unclenched from the first. All week, the practice schedule had been taped to the fridge like liturgy—dates circled in red, margins annotated: Don't forget shin guards. Pack extra water. Be on time.

By Saturday the kitchen hummed like a command center. His mother loaded coolers with the focus of a field medic. His father gave pre-game sermons about hustle and heart like the living embodiment of Coach's echo. Emmalee pirouetted underfoot until Van snapped "Move," and then felt bad for snapping.

Pressure buckled the morning before the keys even left the hook.

At the rec fields, the novelty was gone. Parents unfolded chairs with veteran solemnity. The opposing team warmed up in crisp formation, their movements matching, their confidence loud even before their voices were.

Coach Thomas pulled the boys into a tight huddle. "This one's tougher," he said, voice level with a steel rod through it. "They've got a quick striker. Midfield—apply pressure. Defense—hold your lines. Eyes up. Respect the game. Respect each other."

Van nodded, but the words buzzed like fluorescent lights: there, insistent, hard to absorb. His jersey clung wrong, shin guards itched, cleats pinched. He tried to bounce on his toes like the others. His legs argued with the concept.

Jeremiah slapped his back. "Relax. It's just soccer. Don't over-think it."

Just soccer. If only.

The whistle split the air.

Chaos answered.

Blue jerseys flowed like a tide, passes snapping clean, voices sharp as clicks. Twice Van reached for the ball and lost it to smarter feet. Coach's voice cut from the sideline: "Spread out! Van, watch your wing!"

Heat rushed Van's face. He darted left, then right. The striker slipped past like smoke and turned the field into a runway. Parents' groans rose in one voice. A whistle. One–nil.

Stomach drop. Tight chest.

From the sideline, his father pooled his hands around his mouth. "Hustle, Donovan! You've gotta want it!"

The words bit—familiar teeth.

Jeremiah jogged past, palm landing on Van's shoulder. "Shake it off. Next play." Kind, steady—and carrying the shadow no one ever admits: *Don't drag us down.*

The game wore on, brutal as a treadmill. Van chased, lunged, misread by inches. When the ball came again, he over-swung—sent it skating to nowhere. The groan that followed felt personal.

"Head in the game!" Coach barked, patience thinned.

Van wanted to step off the map. The field felt too wide, the crowd too close, the air rationed.

Meanwhile Jeremiah slipped through it all like a song in the right key. Crisp passes, clean recoveries, quick claps that stitched the team back together. Even his mistakes looked like choices.

Van watched with a cocktail of awe and dread. Same age. Same jersey. Entirely different gravity.

By the final whistle—3–1, loss tallied and stamped—Van's legs had turned to filled sandbags. He bent double, palms on knees, lungs lit with static.

The team crowded into post-game murmurs: bad calls, unlucky bounces, next time. Jeremiah did the captain thing without being called captain—voice even, eyes lifting guys one by one. "One game. We reset."

Van stayed quiet. Words scraped too much to use.

On the walk to the car, his father resumed the sermon. "You can't jog. You've gotta fight. Don't let the ball own you—you own the ball. Understand?"

Van nodded because it's what the world required. Inside, something pinched tighter with each clause. *I am trying* piled up behind his teeth like traffic.

His mother offered soft balm from the driver's seat. "You'll get better with practice. It takes time." Meant as comfort, received as another measurement.

Jeremiah's van rolled past with windows down, music unbothered, laughter spilling like they hadn't just lost. Sun snagged in Jeremiah's hair. He turned to say something to someone and grinned.

Van leaned his head against the glass and watched the grin flicker past like a signal he couldn't catch.

He wondered—not for the first time—how far behind a person could be and still call it the same road.

"Some echoes aren't meant to fade — only to find where they began."

CHAPTER 18

ON DISPLAY

Saturday nights at Heritage Baptist were never really for the teens. The flyers promised "Youth Outings," but the truth rode shotgun in every car: parents—chauffeurs, chaperones, arbiters of when fun had run its course.

Tonight, it was bowling.

Victory Lanes breathed at them like a hot mouth—fryer grease, cheap beer, and the permanent ghost of cigarettes baked into the carpet. Neon strips buzzed overhead, painting the slick lanes in rinses of purple and green. Somewhere in the back, an arcade machine sang a stubborn 8-bit melody, swallowed every few seconds by the crash of pins.

The teens spilled in like they owned the place. Colby "accidentally" asked for shoes two sizes too big, just to needle the rental clerk. Seth hollered at a cluster of rival-team girls campsite'd in a corner booth. Jeremiah leaned at the counter with his effortless smile, blond hair catching the neon until even the middle-aged attendant cracked.

Van kept to the edges. His mother had driven him and Emmalee in the Dodge Caravan, her eyes already tracking the other moms near the snack bar—women with Cokes in paper cups and the hawk-still posture of practiced watchers.

"C'mon, Van!" Colby lobbed a pair of shoes at his chest. "Don't make me carry you."

"Thanks," Van muttered, fumbling the laces. Jeremiah dropped onto the bench beside him, elbow brushing his arm.

"You bowl much?"

"Not really," Van said. "Last time I ended up in the gutter more than the pins."

Jeremiah smirked. "Perfect. Seth bowls like he's pitching hay bales."

"HEY!" Seth bellowed from two lanes over, sending the boys into laughter.

The night found a rhythm—balls thudding, pins scattering, nacho trays tipping, neon reflections sliding across polished boards. Van gutter-balled twice; the groans came on cue; Jeremiah clapped anyway, loud and stubborn. "Hey, it went forward!" Colby added a jab about Seth's windup, and soon Van was laughing too, embarrassment dissolving into the mess.

Parents hovered at a safe distance, their conversations rising and falling like tide—recipes, prayer requests, rumors softened to "concerns." Van tried not to see his mother nodding at all the right places, or his father holding a styrofoam cup like a badge, performing geniality with the other dads.

By the time the parents called it, the scoreboard still blinked unfinished frames. The Davis Suburban idled by the doors; headlights swept the wet asphalt. Van watched Jeremiah and Colby shoulder-bump into the backseat, laughter spilling before the door clicked shut.

"Finally," Van's father grumbled when he slid into the Caravan. "Thought y'all were moving in."

His mother glanced back. "Did you have fun?"

Van's eyes tracked the Suburban's taillights turning onto the road, twin red commas in the dark. "Yeah," he said, soft. "I did."

But as their van rattled after, he felt truth press in: fun didn't change the gravity of things. He was always being carried—by parents, by friends, by a life that jogged two steps faster than his lungs.

MORNING ARRIVED SHARP AND REGIMENTED.

Sunday at the Shelton house was never gentle. Shirts ironed stiff enough to crease skin, hair combed until it stung, ties cinched like vows. His father's voice thundered down the hall: "Let's move! We're not walking in late like heathens. Millie— where's his tie?"

Van stood before the mirror, tugging a knot that wouldn't look like it grew there. His father's reflection filled the doorway.

"That's the tie?" Scoff. "Looks like you're headed to prom with a girl you had to pay for."

Heat crawled Van's neck. Arguing only salted the wound. He finished the knot.

By the time they piled into the Caravan, the air was thick enough to bite. His mother patted lipstick into place using the visor mirror. Emmalee hummed her Sunday School song, doll propped like a parishioner. Van pressed his forehead to the glass; the blur of pines felt kinder than the silence.

The Heritage lot was a pageant: fathers tugging jackets true, mothers ferrying children in pastels, toddlers wailing about bows and shoes. The Davis Suburban gleamed two rows up, wax catching the sun. Jeremiah jumped out first, racing his sisters; his laugh traveled.

"See that?" Van's father said, not bothering to lower his voice. "Now there's a boy who knows how to carry himself. Straight shoulders. Confidence. That's what people respect."

Not an arrow, but it found its mark.

Inside, the vestibule buzzed with perfume and greetings. Aunt Leslie swooped on Millie, linking arms, pulling her toward the sanctuary like a gentle abduction. Van's father clasped hands with deacons; his laugh went brighter, smoother, a polished Sunday version of itself.

By the pew, Van's tie felt like a leash. His father leaned down, a whisper only for him: "Watch yourself. Don't make a scene this time."

From the aisle, they were the picture—father leading, mother shining, children composed. Van sat with the bruise of the whisper throbbing beneath his collar, just another mask in a world already crowded with them.

CHAPTER 19

SUNDAY AT GRANDMA SHELTON'S

Grandma Shelton's house always smelled like time: onions going translucent in butter, ham hocks surrendering to beans, cornbread rising slow in a black-skillet universe. The kitchen clock ticked steady against low talk, older than Van, older than the arguments it sometimes outlasted.

Gatherings "just happened" every so often—though no one ever called them optional. Uncle David and Aunt Leslie were already in place when they arrived; David loosened his tie the moment his mother's back turned; Leslie perched at the counter, sweet tea in hand, wearing the easy air of a woman who knew she was Mama's favorite.

Van followed his parents across the linoleum, clutching his bag. Grandma didn't turn from the stove when she spoke.

"Shoes off, Jeffrey. You weren't raised in a barn."

Jeff froze mid-stride, then toe-flicked his loafers aside like a chastened teenager. For a blink, Van saw it—the boy inside the booming father.

"And David," she added, still not turning, "quit picking at that roast before grace."

David set down the pilfered fork with a grin, caught red-handed. Leslie smothered a smirk in her tea.

The table groaned—butter beans glossed with pot liquor, macaroni casserole freckled brown at the edges, fried chicken stacked like architecture, tomatoes and cucumbers shining with vinegar. Grandma moved through it all with quiet authority: spoon in one hand, cane tucked against the counter; she never needed to raise her voice more than a notch.

Hands linked, heads bowed. Her prayer rolled unhurried, a blessing braided with warning. "Lord, keep us humble at this table, and remind us to use our tongues for kindness, not for sharpness." Van peeked; his father and Uncle David both adjusted in their chairs like schoolboys.

Dinner buzzed. Leslie recounted choir practice melodrama; David inflated a job-site story until it floated; Emmalee hummed nonsense between macaroni spoonfuls. Van ate quiet, but Grandma's gaze missed nothing—his untouched green beans, his father's jaw setting harder, the way Van's shoulders dipped when Jeff's tone sharpened.

"You need something green, sweetheart," she said, sliding the bowl his way. "Your daddy forgets, but I remember twelve. Growing feels heavy sometimes."

Jeff bristled. "He's old enough to clean his plate."

Her eyes clicked to him, calm and direct. "And you were old enough to know better than running off with my Buick at sixteen, but I didn't throw you to the wolves, Jeffrey Allen."

David choked on tea, laughing. Jeff's ears went red. For one breath, the room loosened into joy.

Van ducked his head; a smile tugged. It wasn't only that she defended him—it was that she could reach back and tug his father level with a single remembered rope.

Pie arrived, voices rose. Van leaned back, watching his grandmother settle at the head. She wasn't loud like Sheila, nor soft like

Millie. She carried authority like cast iron—seasoned, steady, unbreakable.

For the first time in a long while, a small safety flickered—like the lamp you leave on in a storm.

CHAPTER 20

CRACKS IN THE FACADE

The Sunday evening cookout was supposed to be casual —burgers on paper plates, kids barefoot in the grass. But even casual at Heritage wore lacquer. Folding tables sagged under crockpots and competition. Lawn chairs circled like thrones for moms sipping sweet tea, their gossip a gentle electric.

On the field's edge, Deacon Thomas worked the grill like a post—spatula snapping, patties flipped with stopwatch precision. Smoke braided upward, making the yard smell like July and memory. Kids chased a soccer ball across patchy grass, laughter skipping higher than the sizzle.

Van hovered by the cooler, excavating a soda just to give his hands a job. Heat stuck his shirt to his back. Across the grass, Jeremiah and Colby jogged into the pickup game, their shouts bright. Jeremiah moved like lines on a map had been drawn for him—shirt clinging, hair damp, laugh unpinned and easy.

Then his father's voice cracked the scene. "Why aren't you out there with them? Afraid to break a nail?"

Chuckles from the dads—a social reflex. Coach Thomas's smile stuttered, then held.

"I'm fine here," Van said to the ice, voice flat.

"Nonsense." His father's hand landed on his shoulder—heavy, guiding. "Go show 'em you've got guts. You're not gonna sit around looking like a bookworm all your life."

Across the grass, like the script had been written, Jeremiah cupped his hands: "We need one more!" The grin—pure invitation.

Behind Van, his father laughed louder for the audience. "That's my boy. Don't let me down."

The game was a pinball machine. The ball skittered across bald patches; kids bounced off each other; rules were mostly wishes. Van chased with legs that already felt tired, missed two easy touches, and then—caught a cleat, met dirt. Laughter rippled, some sharp, some sympathetic.

Jeremiah reached him in a blink, hauling him up. "Shake it off. Happens to everyone." The steadiness in his voice was a handrail.

From the sideline, the punchline followed: "Guess we'll stick him in the goal. At least then he can't trip over himself!"

This time the dads laughed louder. The words sticky as spilled soda.

By burger time, Van's shirt clung with sweat and something he didn't have a name for. He folded into a chair at the crowd's far edge, the unopened soda can sweating against his shoe. At the grill, his father retold the fall like a highlight reel—harmless fun for the men, a fresh bruise for the boy.

The van ride home was padded in thick quiet. Gravel popped under the tires and then smoothed into highway hush. Emmalee slept with her doll's yarn hair stuck to her cheek. Millie held the folded bulletin in her lap like a fragile thing and hummed a tune too soft to catch.

Van pressed his temple to the glass; each breath fogged a circle that vanished before it meant anything.

It didn't take long. His father's voice came low and edged. "You need to toughen up, son. Can't go through life falling on your face every time someone expects you to keep up."

Van watched his own half-lit reflection. Smaller than he felt inside. "I tried," he said, barely.

Laughter—one sharp bark. "Tried? Trying's not cutting it. You think Jeremiah's out there 'trying'? He gets it done. Carries himself like a man. People respect that."

Jeremiah again. Always the measuring stick. Van hated the tiny ember of resentment, hated that it glowed.

Millie turned slightly, gentle steel in her voice. "He's still learning. He did fine."

"Fine?" His father's hands tightened on the wheel; veins rose like cords. "Falling on your butt in front of the whole church is fine now? That's the problem—excuses. 'I tried.'"

Van dug his nails into denim—small half-moons of protest. The words he wanted—I never asked for this—stayed caged for Emmalee's sleep and the shape of his mother's mouth.

"He's not Jeremiah," Millie tried again. "He's Van. And—"

"Exactly," his father snapped. "He's Van. My son. Time to stop hiding in the shadows and act like it."

The sentence landed heavier than the fall itself.

At home, the porch light haloed moths. His father lit a cigarette; the ember pulsed in the dark like an eye. Van slipped inside. The house made its familiar night sounds—the hum of the fridge, the sigh in the pipes. Emmalee padded away, already forgetting the evening.

Van closed his bedroom door and leaned his back against it. Laughter from the cookout rang phantom-loud in his ears, layered with his father's voice until both became one noise.

To the church, they were the Sheltons—neat, smiling, faithful.

In his room's quiet, Van could feel the truth like hairline fractures under a coat of paint.

The cracks were spreading.

CHAPTER 21

THE GAME THAT CHANGED EVERYTHING

The kitchen was dim except for the halo over the table—a circle of light that made everything inside it look official and everything outside feel like shadow. The church newsletter sprawled across the surface, half-buried under a wide-open wall calendar. Millie sat centered like a commander at a war table, pen scratching with the authority of someone writing statutes, not reminders. Each square was already crowded: neat notes, arrows, circles, a lattice of obligation that left almost no white to breathe in.

"Tuesday and Thursday—soccer practice." Her voice came measured, almost liturgical. "Saturday mornings—games. Wednesday night service. Sunday morning *and* evening. Choir rehearsal for Emmalee. Teen lock-in on the fifteenth." She paused, tapped the margin, and added with swift finality: **youth car wash—fundraiser TBD.**

Van hovered in the doorway, bag slipping off his shoulder and thudding against the floor. His legs still hummed with leftover drills, and the sight of the calendar tightened his stomach like a fist. "That's... a lot."

"It's life," his mother said without looking up. "Idle hands don't please God."

From the archway, his father's silhouette shifted—arms crossed, the familiar weight of scrutiny pitched toward him. "You better keep up. No excuses, you hear?"

"Yes, sir," Van said, gravel scraping his throat.

Millie finally lifted her face. A smile tried to reach her eyes and fell short. "We're building something here, Van. Heritage isn't just where we go—it's who we are. It's what will shape you. Don't fight it."

He nodded, eager to escape, and slipped down the hall.

In his room, he fell backward onto the bed and stared up at the slow-circling fan. His father's bark still rang; his mother's pen still scratched across the squares inside his head. Beneath both, Jeremiah's laugh threaded through like a bright wire. It was too much, all of it—and yet under the exhaustion, something small and dangerous flickered like a pilot light: hope.

SATURDAY ARRIVED with July turning the sun into a spotlight. The rec fields shimmered; chain-link fences threw off silver flashes; the grass at center was worn to dirt where cleats had chewed it bare. The air smelled like hot dogs and nacho powder, layered with the aluminum tang of bleachers baking in their own heat.

Parents unfolded chairs in neat rows as if arranging pews, coolers tucked like hymnals at their feet. Fellowship spilled into Saturday: murmured prayers disguised as pep talks, gossip softened to "bless their hearts."

Van tugged at his stiff yellow **HERITAGE BAPTIST** jersey. It clung wrong, more costume than uniform. His cleats felt twice their weight. Across the field, Jeremiah jogged in easy, confident strides—sunlight catching in his blond hair until it looked lit from inside. Colby and Seth were already clowning by the bench, tossing a ball like the game was just the soundtrack to their jokes.

Then came the soft, certain **tap, tap, tap** of a cane on gravel.

"Well, if it isn't my boy, ready to show the world what he's got."

Van turned.

Grandma stood at the bleachers' edge, leaning lightly on her carved cane. Navy skirt, crisp white cardigan, silver hair tight as a promise. Years had been kind to her face, but her eyes—steel gray, clear as winter—missed nothing.

Millie blinked and hurried over. "Mom, I didn't know you were coming."

Grandma lowered herself onto the folding chair Millie tugged out—deliberate, regal. "And let you clap without me? Not a chance. Somebody needs to cheer this boy whether he makes a goal or just stands out there sweatin'."

Jeff shifted in his own chair, jaw flexing. "He doesn't need coddling, Mama. He needs grit."

Her gaze slid sideways—quiet as a blade. "Jeffrey Shelton, don't mistake love for coddling. That boy's wound tighter than a fiddle string already. A little encouragement might do more than all your barking."

Two seats down, Aunt Sheila snorted, sunglasses slipping. She raised her Coke in salute. "Amen to that. Lord knows half these men think hollering from the sidelines is a sport. Van's here to play, not audition for the Marines."

A ripple of chuckles moved the row. Jeff flushed and swallowed whatever came next.

The whistle blew.

The game opened like a jar under pressure. Maroon jerseys crashed against Heritage yellow; the ball skittered and zipped; voices braided into one clamor. Van jogged on stiff legs—lungs burning too soon, every motion amplified by the crowd's noise. Cheers, groans, advice shouted like commandments.

And then—the ball at his feet.

"Go, Van!" Jeremiah's voice cut clean through the clatter—warm, steady, like a hand on the center of his back.

For a heartbeat he froze. A defender charged; cleats pounded thunder into the ground. Panic stood up in him, ready to yank the plug.

Something deeper stood taller.

He faked left, darted right, planted, swung.

The ball left his foot with a sweet, hollow *thunk*—clean, truer than he'd felt all season. It sailed on a rising line. The keeper lunged—fingertips grazing—too late.

Net. Bulge. A crisp inhale from the crowd—then detonation.

Bleachers erupted: claps, whistles, the bright off-key choir of victory. Seth bellowed like he'd witnessed the northern lights. Colby punched the sky hard enough to hurt later. Jeremiah turned, fist raised, grin wide and fierce—pride burning clear in his eyes.

Van's chest heaved. For once, the air came in as if it belonged to him.

Grandma clapped slow and royal, smile opening like a door. Aunt Sheila's whistle split the heat sharper than the ref's. Millie pressed her hands together under her chin, half laugh, half prayer.

Jeff stayed seated, arms crossed, mouth a hard line.

Grandma turned her head, pitched her voice so every nearby parent could hear. "That's your boy. First time he's kicked that ball into that fishing-net basket thing. Don't you dare rob him of this moment. He's practically ready for the Super Bowl."

Jeff muttered, "It's called a goal, Mother, not—"

Her eyes flashed. "Don't you correct me. It's a *goal basket,* and it's the best one I've seen today."

Parents around them chuckled. Aunt Sheila grinned like she'd just cashed a ticket. "Preach, Mama Shelton."

Van ducked his head, smiling into his collar. For once, the correction didn't land on him.

Play resumed, but the field had changed shape. Not the chalk lines—the feeling. Drills, bruises, the long week of being measured—none of it mattered in the handful of heartbeats after the net rippled. Jeremiah's palm thumped Van's back, lingered a breath longer than habit. His grin held steady; his steel-blue eyes sparked with a something Van couldn't name and didn't dare to.

For a moment brief as a coin toss, Van let himself believe he had done something irrefutably right.

Then, across the field, his father's gaze found him again—unmoved, unsmiling. The old weight settled where it always did, the familiar bar across his ribs.

But underneath that weight, the pilot light didn't go out. It steadied. It burned.

CHAPTER 22

CRACKS IN THE FOUNDATION

The gymnasium smelled like fried chicken and Lysol—a scent so deeply woven into Heritage Baptist that it might as well have been part of the doctrine. Folding tables bowed under the weight of casseroles, crockpots, and cakes the size of hymnals, while the silent basketball hoops loomed above like watchful sentinels. The noise—laughter, chatter, the scrape of chairs—was supposed to sound like comfort. Tonight, it didn't.

Van sat at the end of one table, paper plate balanced on his knees. He'd filled it the way he always did—barbecue, baked beans, one of Mrs. Abernathy's deviled eggs—but none of it looked edible. His stomach was still tangled from the game, from the cheer that had turned to silence, from the words his father had lobbed like stones on the drive over.

Across from him, Colby reenacted a slide tackle that had left his leg streaked with mud, windmilling his arms for emphasis. Seth laughed so hard his Styrofoam cup trembled, sweet tea sloshing over the rim. Jeremiah clapped Colby's shoulder, adding commentary that made the story grow taller with each retelling. They looked *whole* together—boys who fit, unbothered, untouchable.

Van tore his dinner roll into smaller and smaller pieces, pretending to listen, pretending to belong.

"Why aren't you eating?"

His father's voice dropped low but cut sharp enough to slice through the chatter.

"Not that hungry," Van murmured.

"Not that hungry," Jeff repeated, louder this time—just enough for heads to turn. "You scored a goal today, and you can't even stomach supper? What kind of sense does that make?"

Heat flared under Van's skin. The bread in his hands collapsed into damp crumbs. He forced a forkful of beans into his mouth, swallowing hard against the taste.

"Jeff."

The word came steady as a bell, carrying clear across the table.

Grandma.

It was the first thing she'd said since sitting down, but her presence had already commanded the space. She sat upright, posture proud, her silver hair pinned back with pearl combs that winked under the fluorescent lights. Her dress was simple navy, her shoes sensible, but her eyes—steel-gray, unblinking—cut through the noise like scripture.

"You're embarrassing yourself more than him," she said evenly, gaze fixed on her son. "That boy played hard today. I saw it with my own eyes. That was no 'lucky kick.' That was *effort*."

Jeff's jaw flexed. "I'm trying to push him to do better."

"Push him," she said, "but don't shove him under water and then act surprised when he can't breathe."

The table went still. Even Colby stopped mid-sentence. The only sound was the hum of the overhead lights.

Van froze, fork halfway to his mouth. The words landed deep—something he'd never been brave enough to say himself.

Jeff leaned back, crossing his arms tighter. "He needs grit."

"And he needs encouragement," Grandma countered, voice

softening without losing weight. "One without the other is cruelty, son."

Van's throat burned. He stared at the beans swimming in sauce, but then a hand—cool, firm—slipped over his. Grandma's. Her grip was small but anchoring, a kind of strength that didn't shout to be heard.

"You did well today, Van," she said, her voice just for him now. "Don't let anyone—" her eyes flicked toward Jeff "—steal that from you."

His vision blurred. He nodded, swallowing the lump in his chest until it went down whole.

Across the table, his mother sat frozen, fork hovering above her plate. Her eyes shifted between her son and her mother-in-law, something flickering there—longing, envy, maybe both. Millie Shelton wasn't weak; she just didn't wear her strength in steel. She wore it in silence, in smoothing edges, in surviving her husband's certainty. But tonight, she wished she had her mother-in-law's fire.

When Van looked up, Millie met his eyes. Her smile was small and wet, a quiet translation: *I wish I could give you what she gives.*

The air held still for one trembling beat—until Aunt Shelia's voice detonated from the next table.

"Well, if that ain't the pot callin' the kettle black!"

Laughter burst around her like popcorn. "Jeff, you struttin' around here like you're Coach of the Year when the only thing you're coachin' is how to wear a belt two sizes too small!"

The nearby tables erupted. Jeff's neck went crimson. Shelia didn't flinch—she never did. Her bracelets clinked as she raised her fork like a gavel.

"You want grit? Try raisin' kids without actin' like Sunday morning's Broadway. Church ain't about struttin' for applause— it's about livin' it when nobody's watchin'. And I ain't seen you do much of that lately."

"Shelia," Millie warned, but her tone carried a thread of laughter.

"What? I'm just sayin' what everyone's thinkin'," Shelia said, lifting her Coke in mock toast. "And thank the Lord somebody's sayin' it, 'cause y'all Shelton men sure do love the sound of your own sermons."

The table rippled with nervous chuckles. Jeff muttered something sharp under his breath and turned to his plate. The sting still hung in the air.

Grandma gave Shelia the faintest nod, then turned back to Van. She squeezed his hand one more time before letting go, letting him return to his plate with shoulders that didn't feel like armor.

He took another bite. The barbecue was lukewarm, the beans still sweet, the deviled egg too tangy—but for the first time all evening, the food didn't taste like punishment.

It tasted like belonging. Like maybe, just maybe, someone at this table saw him—not the perfect son, not the sermon prop, but *him.*

And that realization settled somewhere new inside him—not as a wound this time, but as a seed.

"They said God made us in His image. No one mentioned how heavy the mirror would be."

CRACKS AT HOME

The Shelton house carried its usual Sunday rhythm—plates clinking, the low hum of conversation, the faint hiss of the oven cooling—but tonight it felt brittle. One wrong word, one fork scrape too loud, and the whole fragile calm might split apart.

The table was set the way Millie always set it—baked chicken, green beans, and her biscuits, soft and steaming, like comfort she kept trying to serve into existence. The smell should have been home. Instead, it hung in the air like a cover for something sour beneath.

Van sat at the far end, shoulders rounded, dragging his fork through his beans in slow, absent circles. His stomach still twisted from the game—from his father's voice echoing over the bleachers, from the car ride that had been one long sermon on toughness. Across from him, Emmalee swung her legs, humming "Jingle Bells" though it was nowhere near December, feeding her doll imaginary bites and giggling to herself, a whole world away from the tension that kept the table stiff.

Jeff Shelton sat at the head, a fixture carved from impatience, arms crossed, eyes trained on Van's plate.

"You barely touched your food," he said, low but edged enough to cut through Millie's gentle chatter.

"Not really hungry," Van murmured.

"Not hungry," Jeff repeated, louder this time, until even Emmalee's tune stuttered out. "You ran that field like you were dragging a plow. You need muscle. You want to stay a string bean your whole life?"

The words hit harder than the whistle at the game. Van's chest burned. He opened his mouth, but before the defense could crawl out, another voice sliced clean across the table.

"Jeffrey Shelton."

Grandma.

She was there tonight—a rare presence at supper. Lavender cardigan, floral blouse, silver hair swept into a perfect bun. The light caught her pearl combs when she turned her head, glinting like punctuation to every truth she spoke. She didn't raise her voice; she never needed to. Still, the air shifted around her.

"Don't tear him down when he's already tired," she said calmly. "You don't build strength by breaking the spirit that carries it."

Jeff's jaw flexed. For a fleeting second, under her gaze, he looked almost young—like the boy who'd once been scolded at this same table. "I'm not tearing him down, Mama. I'm teaching him grit."

Her tone softened, but the steel stayed. "Then teach it with encouragement. Otherwise, it's cruelty dressed up as parenting."

Silence draped the room, heavy as humidity. Van felt something loosen in his ribs—a small crack where air could finally get in.

Then, from the far end, Emmalee piped up, bright and earnest.

"I think Van's strong already. He carried me on his back all the way up Grandma's hill last week." She beamed, doll clutched to her chest. "He only huffed a little."

Laughter bubbled around the table, unexpected and contagious. Even Jeff's mouth twitched toward a reluctant smile before he cleared his throat. Millie seized the moment like a lifeline.

"See? The boy's not lazy. He's got more in him than you give him credit for."

Her voice wasn't sharp—but it carried something new, a quiet defiance that startled even her. Jeff gave her a long look, the kind meant to end the discussion, then turned back to his plate.

The rest of the meal unfolded in uneasy truce—forks scraping, plates clinking, Emmalee's humming filling the gaps no one else could.

LATER THAT WEEK, the gym buzzed under fluorescent light—the same hum as always, the same half-warm scent of rubber and floor polish. Youth group chaos sprawled in every direction. Teens clustered around the snack table, traded inside jokes, shot hoops that clanged more than they scored. Faded posters hung on the cinderblock walls: **Stand Firm in the Faith. Run the Race. Finish Strong.** Their corners curled, like even they were tired.

Jeremiah stood in the middle of it all, laughter orbiting him the way light does a flame. Colby leaned in, loud and easy, teasing Seth about his so-called "farm-boy strength." The group swelled around them—comfortable, unguarded.

Van hovered at the edge, hands buried in his hoodie pockets, watching and wishing he knew the choreography of belonging.

Jeremiah noticed first. "Hey, Shelton!" he called, grinning. "Come on—help us settle this. Who sings worse, Brother Andy or Miss Gwen?"

Colby cackled. "Bro Andy, easy. Man sounds like a lawn mower starting in January."

Even Van laughed, sliding onto the bleacher beside them. For a few minutes, he forgot about the rest—the field, the lectures, the weight that usually came with his last name. The laughter felt warm, ordinary, almost like safety.

Then the gym doors groaned open.

Jeff Shelton stepped inside.

He wasn't supposed to be there. But there he was, arms crossed, scanning the room until his gaze found his son.

"Van!" he barked. "Why aren't you practicing shots? You've got plenty to improve!"

The laughter died mid-breath. Heads turned. The air tightened.

Jeremiah leaned in, muttering, "Ignore him. Stay put."

But Jeff stayed where he was—leaning on the doorframe like a man waiting for proof. Authority radiated off him like heat.

Van stood, throat dry, grabbed a basketball, and sent it ricocheting off the rim with a clang so bad it didn't even kiss the backboard. A few kids snickered quietly. Jeff smirked like the moment had been staged just to make his point, then left without another word.

Silence lingered behind him until Jeremiah clapped Van's shoulder. "Forget him. We're not the NBA."

Van smiled thinly, but the sting sat heavy in his chest.

THAT NIGHT, the kitchen smelled of dish soap and damp towels. The clink of plates punctuated Millie's quiet fury as she dried and stacked them with unnecessary care. Jeff leaned against the counter, arms crossed, voice dripping with certainty.

"You embarrassed him," she said finally, breaking the hum. "Marching into that gym, calling him out in front of everyone— what did that do but humiliate him?"

Jeff scoffed. "It showed him he can't hide. If he's gonna be there, he better earn it."

"He *was* earning it," she said, turning to face him now. Her tone didn't rise, but it sharpened. "You just can't see it because it doesn't look like you think it should. Maybe it's not the field he belongs on. Maybe it's somewhere else."

Jeff's expression hardened. "Sports build character. They make boys into men."

"Or they break them down," she said softly, almost sadly.

From the hallway, Van stood frozen, back pressed to the wallpaper, his heartbeat pounding loud in his ears. He could barely breathe. Hearing his mother—his gentle, careful mother—stand up like that felt like watching a wall shift out of place. It was terrifying. And it was beautiful.

Later, in his room, the house gone quiet, Van lay staring at the ceiling. The words replayed over and over—his grandmother's steel, his mother's spark.

He exhaled, slow, almost a prayer.

"Thank you."

CHAPTER 24

WORDS THAT STICK

The weekend came dressed in routine—church bulletins, casserole dishes, the rustle of Sunday dresses—but the air shifted the moment Grandma announced she'd be joining again.

She hadn't been to youth games in years. "Too much noise," she always said. But that morning, she arrived with her lavender cardigan buttoned neat, her silver hair swept up like a crown, cane tucked under one arm though she barely leaned on it.

"I figured it was time I came and saw my grandson play more," she said as she settled into the van beside Emmalee, who hugged her hard enough to nearly tip her purse over. "Besides, y'all make so much fuss about soccer, I might as well see what the Lord's been braggin' about."

The humor sparkled, but her eyes—steady and gray as river stone—met Van's. A small, knowing smile. *I'm here for you.*

The rec field buzzed with familiar chaos: chairs pitched at crooked angles, hot dogs sizzling, kids shrieking over melted snow cones. The air shimmered with sun and chatter and the faint metallic rattle of bleachers.

Van jogged through warm-ups, but his body felt rigid, his

father's stare pressing down from the sidelines like a weight he couldn't shake. Jeremiah jogged past, slapping his shoulder. "Relax. It's just a game."

But Van already heard the echo of his father's voice in his head—*Plant your feet. Don't just stand there. Move.*

And then, slicing through the noise, came a voice that didn't sound like correction but like freedom.

"Go on, Van! Show them how it's done!"

Heads turned. Parents chuckled. A few smiled.

Van's ears burned crimson—but under the flush, warmth spread through him like light seeping under a closed door. Nobody had ever cheered for him like that. Not once.

Jeremiah grinned. "Looks like you've got your own fan club."

"She's embarrassing," Van muttered. But he couldn't stop the grin that crept up anyway.

THE GAME UNFOLDED the usual way—Jeremiah brilliant, Colby reckless, Van scrambling to stay in the rhythm. He missed one block, then another. His father's voice cut through the crowd.

"Plant your feet, Van! What are you doing?"

The sting was immediate, but before it could settle, another voice answered—sharp, sure, commanding:

"He's doing just fine, Jeff! Let the boy play!"

The entire sideline stilled. A few parents smirked behind their hands. Jeff's face went stone-hard.

Van stood frozen mid-field, heart pounding. Jeremiah caught his eye, grinning wide. "Your grandma's a legend," he whispered.

Van laughed despite himself. The sound felt brand new.

AFTER THE FINAL WHISTLE, while Coach Thomas rattled off his notes, Grandma waited by the fence. She waved him over, cane balanced against her knee.

"You played just fine," she said, cupping his cheek in her palm. Her touch was cool, firm. "Don't you let your daddy tell you otherwise."

Van swallowed, voice barely there. "I'm not good at it."

"Maybe not yet," she said, eyes bright and fierce. "But life's not about being good at everything. It's about standing your ground when people tell you you're less than you are. And you did that today. I saw it."

The words rooted deep, strong and quiet as bedrock. He nodded, blinking too fast to stop the heat in his eyes.

Millie approached then, Emmalee tugging her hand, babbling about snow cones. She stopped short when she saw them—her mother's hand resting on Van's shoulder, the boy leaning into it without shame. Something flickered in Millie's eyes—longing, maybe, or recognition.

"You two look thick as thieves," she teased, though her voice trembled.

Grandma chuckled. "This one's got more fire than people see. He just needs folks to stop stomping it out."

Millie smiled, wet-eyed. "She's right," she said softly.

And for a fleeting, fragile moment, they stood as three—a lineage of strength that had taken different shapes: iron, patience, and the quiet resilience of a boy learning to breathe.

Around them, the world kept spinning—Jeremiah teasing Seth, Colby chasing Emmalee, parents folding chairs, the field already fading toward dusk—but inside that small circle of women and boy, something had shifted.

Van didn't feel hidden.

Didn't feel small.

He felt *seen*.

And maybe, for the first time, that was enough.

CHAPTER 25

PRESSURE POINTS

By the third week of games, the Heritage boys had found something close to rhythm. The chaos had quieted into something that almost resembled teamwork. The chalk lines that once felt like traps now looked like invitations—boundaries Van was finally learning to move within. His lungs didn't burn as quickly, his feet no longer fought the ground. Mistakes still happened, but they didn't swallow him whole anymore.

Saturday arrived under a pitiless July sun, the heat rolling off the grass in shimmering waves. The air smelled of cut grass, concession hot dogs, and plastic coolers warming too fast. Folding chairs lined the field like pews, filled with parents fanning themselves with church bulletins, their encouragement ringing out like a Sunday revival.

Van squinted against the glare, the yellow of his HERITAGE BAPTIST jersey nearly blinding. He'd been slotted on defense again—safe, steady, where mistakes didn't draw as much blood. But today, something inside him buzzed. A restless energy. A need to prove, maybe to himself, maybe to someone watching.

The whistle blew. The game lurched to life.

Midway through the first half, a forward twice his size came barreling toward him, cleats pounding the earth like thunder. Van braced, heart hammering. The ball spun between them—a blur of white and dirt—and instinct took over. He lunged, met the ball clean, and stole it away before the other boy could blink.

Gasps from the sideline. A flash of disbelief from the opposing player. Then the crowd erupted.

"That's it, Van! Good job, son!"

The voice cut through the noise.

His father.

Not mocking. Not biting. Not another bark of correction. Just proud.

The sound hit harder than the sun. For a heartbeat, Van forgot to breathe. The ball flew downfield, forgotten under the weight of that single word—*son.*

Jeremiah jogged past, grin easy and radiant. "Look at you, Shelton. Getting some respect."

Van's pulse stumbled. Respect. From him. From both of them. He could've floated off the field if gravity hadn't been holding him down.

Even later—after the final whistle, after Grandma declared to every listening ear, *"Didn't I say? Tougher than he knows!"*—his father clapped a heavy hand on his back, knocking him forward a step.

"That's more like it," Jeff said. Gruff, but real.

And that was enough. For once, the praise didn't come wrapped in a lesson. It just… was.

Van couldn't stop smiling. Not even when Emmalee spilled cherry snow-cone syrup down his jersey, leaving a pink stain like a victory badge.

The team crowded near the bleachers, laughter swelling in waves. Seth bragged about a goal he almost made, Colby shoved Jeremiah into a headlock, and everyone roared like the world had tilted just right. For once, Van wasn't standing on the edge looking in—he was laughing with them, part of the noise instead of swallowed by it.

Then—

"So, Jeremiah…"

Daphne.

Her voice floated across the group, honeyed but deliberate. She'd been part of the youth group forever—the kind of girl who always seemed to be where the spotlight landed. Her curls bounced when she laughed, her nails matched her pastel cardigan, and she wielded her charm like a sharpened Sunday smile.

"When are you going to ask someone out?" she teased, a saccharine lilt beneath the words. "You're practically the prince of Heritage, and all these girls are waiting."

The group howled. Seth elbowed him, Colby smirked. "Yeah, man, Daphne's not subtle."

"She's already monogramming your towels," someone added.

Jeremiah laughed, easy and unbothered—but his ears flushed pink. "I'm focusing on soccer. We're only three games in. That's all I've got time for."

Daphne tilted her head, lashes fluttering. "Everybody makes time for what matters."

The teasing rolled louder, like thunderclouds building, and Jeremiah just laughed again—shoulders loose, grin confident. But then, for one quick second, his eyes flicked toward Van. A glance small enough to miss but sharp enough to cut. Apologetic. Unspoken. Gone.

Van dropped his gaze, scuffing the gravel with his cleat. The noise around him dimmed. His chest felt hollow and tight all at once, like someone had pressed their thumb right into the center of it.

That evening, the Shelton kitchen glowed warm with lamplight and chili simmering on the stove. Aunt Shelia sat perched at the counter, one slipper kicked off, fanning herself with the church bulletin. Millie dried dishes beside her, the clink of porcelain soft against the hum of the air conditioner.

"Can you believe those girls?" Millie said, shaking her head. "Poor Jeremiah can't take a step without Daphne circling him."

Shelia barked a laugh. "That girl? Lord, I've seen smaller dogs beg for scraps with more dignity."

"Shelia," Millie scolded lightly, but her lips twitched.

Grandma stirred her tea, one silver brow raised. "Jeremiah's handsome, and the pastor's son. Girls think catching him's a blessing. But blessings," she said, voice lowering just enough to still the room, "aren't always what they look like."

The silence that followed wasn't awkward—it was knowing. Jeff cleared his throat. "He'll handle himself."

But Van caught the look his grandmother sent him across the table—subtle, soft, seeing. A small smile that said she understood something no one else did.

THE NEXT WEEK, Daphne's laughter seemed to follow them everywhere—trailing Jeremiah through the gym, curling through youth group halls like a perfume. She sat beside him at devotionals, leaned close at snack time, brushed his sleeve when she didn't need to.

The other boys fed the flames, teasing louder each day. "She's already naming your kids!" Seth crowed once, earning a chorus of snickers.

Jeremiah rolled his eyes, playing along with a grin. But every now and then—just when the laughter peaked—he'd glance toward Van. Brief, quiet, like an apology that never reached his lips.

Colby noticed. Colby *always* noticed.

He dropped onto the bleachers beside Van one night, sweat darkening the collar of his jersey. "Don't sweat it, man. Girls like her? All drama. Stick with the ones who've got your back."

He clapped Van's shoulder—firm, grounding. His hand lingered a fraction longer than necessary.

Van froze, pulse skittering, the air between them suddenly charged. He forced a laugh, though his throat was tight. "Yeah."

The word came hollow. Thin.

Because even as Colby's warmth stayed on his shoulder, Van's eyes drifted to Jeremiah—still laughing, still magnetic, still impossibly out of reach.

And somewhere inside him, the pressure built.

The kind that didn't come from the field, or his father, or even the weight of expectation.

It came from the fault lines no one else could see—

and he wasn't sure how much longer he could keep them from cracking.

CHAPTER 26

THE SOUNDS BETWEEN WORDS

The Shelton minivan rattled down the two-lane road that wound between pines and soybean fields, the headlights carving tunnels through the heavy dark. The windows fogged with the breath of four tired bodies, and the hum of the engine filled every space that conversation couldn't.

Emmalee licked syrup from her wrist where her snow cone had melted, the red stain trailing down her arm like war paint. She hummed some tuneless melody that didn't match the radio, her doll buckled safely beside her in a booster seat that had long since outgrown her size. The sound should have been sweet. Instead, it just made the silence louder.

Jeff Shelton drove with one hand on the wheel, the other drumming against his thigh as if he were keeping time to a song only he could hear. "Finally saw some grit out there," he said after a long stretch of nothing, his voice even but clipped, like praise was a muscle he hadn't stretched in years. "About time you played like you meant it."

The words came like something tossed instead of offered.

Van stared out the window, his reflection faint against the blur of pine trees and distant porch lights. He nodded once, hoping that was enough. It should have been a victory—his father hadn't barked, hadn't mocked, hadn't told him to toughen up or stop embarrassing himself. But the praise still carried the same sharp edge it always did, wrapped in expectation. A compliment with conditions attached.

His mother turned slightly in her seat, catching his eyes in the rearview mirror. Her smile was soft, careful, like she wanted to plant something gentle in him before the sharpness took root. "We're proud of you," she said, her voice steady but quiet. "Don't forget that."

Before Van could answer, another voice rose from the back seat—calm, commanding, the kind of voice that stopped conversations midair.

"I'll tell you what I saw," his grandmother said, her words cutting through the hum of tires on asphalt. She sat beside Emmalee, her cane resting against her knee, silver hair glowing faintly in the dashboard light. "I saw a boy stand his ground. I saw him fight past fear and play anyway. That's not luck—that's grit with heart. Don't let anyone tell you different."

Jeff's jaw flexed, his hand tightening on the steering wheel. He didn't argue. He never did when his mother spoke like that. He just pressed harder on the accelerator until the engine's whine filled the van.

Van swallowed, his throat thick. His father said grit. His grandmother said heart. Both felt like languages he didn't quite speak. Praise always came like this—fleeting, contradictory, heavy. It never stayed long enough to settle. Only the weight remained.

By the time the van turned into the driveway, the night had folded in on itself. The porch light blinked twice before flickering out completely, as if even the house knew better than to expect peace to last.

. . .

WEDNESDAY NIGHTS at Heritage Baptist were louder than Sundays —less reverent, more restless. The air in the gym smelled of floor wax and nacho cheese, that strange blend of sacred and snack bar. Folding chairs screeched against the tile as teenagers dragged them into crooked rows. A few kids argued over who got the last can of Dr Pepper from the concession counter, their voices bouncing off the high ceiling like ricochets.

Van trailed behind Jeremiah and Colby, clutching his Bible to his chest like a shield. His mother's reminder—"Be social, Van. It's good for you"—still echoed in his ears. He wasn't sure if it was advice or an order.

Pastor Rich stood at the front, one hand raised to still the crowd, his voice booming over the chatter. "Tonight, we're talking about purity—purity of heart, purity of thought, purity of spirit." His cadence carried the rhythm of a sermon he'd preached a dozen times before. The words floated above the room, only half-catching on restless minds already elsewhere.

Van tried to listen, but his attention kept drifting. Two rows ahead, Daphne sat with her chin resting on her hand, her perfect curls gleaming under the fluorescent lights. She looked up at the pulpit now and then, nodding at the right moments, but her gaze always found its way back to Jeremiah. Her smile was the kind that asked for attention and always got it.

Jeremiah didn't seem to notice—at least not at first. But every so often, he shifted, laughter catching awkwardly in his throat when she leaned a little too close during the opening prayer.

When the devotional ended and the teens scattered for small groups, the whispers started like static in a radio.

"She's totally into him."

"Pastor's son and the prettiest girl in youth group? Kinda obvious."

"You think they're dating yet?"

Van didn't move. He kept his Bible open in his lap, staring at the page without reading a word. The letters swam, black ink against cream paper, blurry with heat and humiliation that wasn't even his to own.

Jeremiah, good-natured as ever, laughed when Seth nudged him and said, "So, when's the wedding?" The grin came easy, but Van caught the flicker behind it—the flash of discomfort before Jeremiah's charm slid back into place.

Then came basketball—the unspoken ritual that followed every service.

The squeak of sneakers replaced the hymns, and the laughter rose again. Jeremiah tossed Van a grin and a ball. "You're on my team, Shelton. No excuses."

The game was chaos. Seth fouled half the time, Colby moved like a linebacker pretending to be graceful, and Jeremiah glided through it all, his movements fluid and unbothered. Van hovered at the edge until a pass came his way. Panic sparked—then instinct took over. He threw the ball.

It arced through the air, hit the rim once, and dropped clean through the net.

The gym erupted. "Look at Van!" Colby shouted, almost tripping from laughing so hard. Jeremiah grabbed him in a quick side hug, ruffling his hair. "See? Told you. You're better than you think."

For a moment, Van's chest filled with something light and electric, like maybe belonging was possible.

Then Daphne's voice sliced through the noise.

"Nice shot, Van," she called, her tone syrupy sweet. "But Jeremiah, aren't you supposed to *carry* the team, not babysit it?"

The laughter that followed wasn't cruel on purpose—it was worse. It was casual. Careless.

Jeremiah's smile faltered. His jaw tensed. Van's face burned hot enough to sting.

Colby muttered under his breath, "Ignore her. Girl thinks the world turns just because she blinks." His hand brushed Van's shoulder in quick reassurance before he jogged downcourt.

The gesture was small. But it anchored him.

WHEN THE GAME ENDED, the noise softened to murmurs. Folding chairs screeched again as they were dragged back into order. Van lingered near the snack table, fingers picking at the label of a water bottle until it shredded in curls on the floor.

The steady click of his grandmother's cane reached him before her voice did. She moved slowly but deliberately, her silver hair pinned in its usual neat twist, her eyes taking in the whole room before resting on him. Aunt Sheila trailed behind her, a Styrofoam cup in hand and a storm already brewing behind her smile.

"Young lady's got eyes too big for her stomach," Grandma said, nodding toward Daphne, who was now laughing loudly near the exit. "Thinks being bold makes her special. But real special doesn't need to scream for attention."

Van looked up, startled by her precision. "I don't think Jeremiah even notices me anymore."

Her eyes softened. "Then that's his mistake, not yours."

Before he could answer, Aunt Sheila's voice boomed across the gym. "Lord have mercy, are y'all seeing this circus? That girl's about to strangle him with those cardigan strings, and everyone's acting like it's prom night."

"Shelia, hush," Millie murmured nearby, stacking paper cups.

"I'll hush when I'm wrong," Sheila said, taking another loud sip. "Church courting's just another kind of show. God's not keeping score for applause."

Grandma smiled faintly. "For once, I agree with her."

Van bit back a laugh, though it came out shaky.

When Jeremiah finally broke free from Daphne and crossed the gym, his grin was back but strained. "Man, she's relentless," he said, rubbing the back of his neck.

"Yeah," Colby added, half-laughing, half-exasperated. "And everyone's eating it up."

Jeremiah glanced at Van, a flash of apology in his eyes. "Sorry, Shelton. You know I'd rather hang with you guys."

Van smiled, but the corners didn't quite reach his eyes. "It's fine."

They stepped out into the cool night, the air damp with the smell of cut grass and rain that never came. Behind them, Daphne's laughter echoed through the gym doors, bright and hollow.

LATER THAT NIGHT, the house was quiet except for the groan of old pipes and the hum of the refrigerator. Van sat hunched at the family computer in the kitchen, the dial-up modem screeching like a trapped bird before finally connecting. The yellow bulb above the sink flickered, painting everything in sickly gold.

His AIM buddy list blinked awake.

xXChurchChicXx has signed on. Daphne.

JereDavis11 is online. Jeremiah.

A chime. A message.

> good game ;)

Van stared at the screen. Was it teasing? Pity? Flirting? He typed "thx," deleted it, typed it again, deleted it once more. His hands trembled slightly.

A few seconds later, Jeremiah's status updated:

BRB – AIMing someone important.

The typing indicator blinked beside Jeremiah's name, steady and constant, then shifted into the "active chat" column—somewhere else. Not him.

Van clicked **Sign Off.**

The computer made that small, hollow *door-slam* sound. The kind that meant goodbye.

The kitchen was silent again except for the low hum of the refrigerator. The alien plush in his backpack pressed against his leg like a secret he wasn't sure he wanted anymore.

He sat there, staring at the dark screen long after it went blank, his reflection faint in the glass—eyes tired, mouth tight.

Outside, the cicadas screamed into the night, filling the silence with sound.

And for the first time since the season began, Van realized how loud being unseen could really be.

CHAPTER 27

SATURDAY SIDELINES

The Saturday morning sky was restless, clouds dragging like gray curtains across a half-lit sun. The air carried the wet weight of July humidity, thick enough to cling to skin and slow every breath. Even before the first whistle, the recreation field throbbed with motion—coolers thumping onto the grass, folding chairs unfolding with sharp metallic snaps, parents fanning themselves with church bulletins as if trying to summon a breeze.

Children darted across the sidelines in bright jerseys, laughter clashing with the bark of coaches and the whine of whistles. The smell of concession-stand popcorn tangled with sunscreen and powdered sugar, and somewhere behind it all came the slow hum of gossip—mothers trading casseroles and commentary in equal measure.

The Shelton minivan rattled into the gravel lot late, its muffler coughing like an old smoker's laugh. Dust billowed behind it, swirling into the hot air. Van sat rigid in the back seat, his shin guards biting into his calves, the yellow **HERITAGE** jersey sticking to his back like a warning sign. His father's jaw worked wordlessly for a moment before the familiar tone hit.

"Come on, Van, hustle. You're not gonna drag your feet before the game even starts."

The sliding door shrieked open. Van grabbed his bag, muttering, "Yes, sir," though his voice barely reached the ground. He tried to fold himself into the stream of families moving toward the field—just another blur of motion and color.

His grandmother was already there. She sat beneath a wide-brimmed straw hat that made her look almost regal, a queen surveying her kingdom from the sidelines. Her cane leaned against the armrest of her folding chair, her eyes sharp enough to see everything worth noticing. Beside her, Aunt Sheila stood with one hand on her hip, narrating the chaos with the practiced ease of a front-porch commentator.

"You'd think this was the World Cup," she announced to no one in particular, loud enough for everyone to hear. "Half these folks act like hollering from the fence is a spiritual gift."

"Shelia," Millie hissed, tugging Emmalee closer by the arm.

"What? Tell me I'm wrong," Sheila shot back, smirking into her Coke can.

On the field, the drills were already underway. Colby sprinted like he was powered by something stronger than oxygen, teal jersey streaked with sweat. Jeremiah jogged with that easy, unhurried rhythm that made even his warm-ups look like highlight reels.

The girls on the bleachers were already watching—Daphne, perfectly centered, leading the synchronized giggles that followed every flick of Jeremiah's hair or grin over his shoulder. Her pink cardigan caught the sunlight like a flag, her laughter echoing with purpose.

"Van!" Coach Thomas's whistle split the air. "Warm-up lap! Move it!"

Van broke into a jog, cleats chewing at the dirt. Jeremiah slid beside him effortlessly, grinning sideways. "Just match me. Don't overthink it."

Van tried. His breath came sharp and uneven, his stride half a beat off. Still, for a brief moment, it worked. Their rhythm found each other. Step for step. Breath for breath.

Then came the voice from the fence.

"Pick up your knees, Van! You look like you're chasing chickens out there!"

Laughter rippled down the line of parents—quick, nervous, and sharper than any whistle.

Van stumbled, nearly clipping Colby, who caught his arm. "Ignore it," Colby muttered, voice firm but low. "You're fine."

Jeremiah's head turned briefly toward the fence. His smile thinned. "Forget them. Stay with me."

Van forced a nod, his chest burning more from shame than heat.

THE WHISTLE SHRIEKED AGAIN, and the game began.

The maroon team opened strong, their passes sharp and calculated, their coordination polished. Within minutes, Heritage was under pressure. Van locked into position on defense, his heart hammering in rhythm with the thudding ball.

A forward—taller, faster—charged straight for him. Van froze for half a heartbeat, then something in him clicked. He lunged, cutting across the player's path. The impact jolted through his legs as the ball ricocheted off his shin and spun wide toward midfield.

Cheers erupted.

"Yes, Van!" Jeremiah's voice cut clear across the chaos. He clapped him hard on the back, laughter bright and genuine.

Van's lungs filled like he'd just surfaced from underwater. Pride—real pride—lit behind his ribs.

And then came the inevitable follow-up.

"'Bout time you did something right!"

His father's voice sliced through the noise like a rusted blade.

The cheers faltered, replaced by quiet murmurs. Van's shoulders folded inward as he jogged back into position, head low. The pride vanished, leaving only the echo.

HALFTIME CAME LIKE MERCY. The team slumped onto the bench, drenched and gasping. Coach barked about hustle and formation, but the words washed past Van in a blur of sound. Jeremiah dropped down beside him, sweat glistening across his temple.

"You're solid today," he said, voice calm. "Don't let it get in your head."

Before Van could answer, another voice—shrill, sweet, and unmistakable—broke through the crowd.

"Jeremiah! Don't drink too much—you'll get a cramp!"

Daphne.

Her laughter was joined by a chorus of giggles from the bleachers. Jeremiah raised his water bottle in mock salute. "Thanks for the advice, Coach," he called, forcing a grin.

Colby groaned beside Van. "She's exhausted," he muttered, voice dripping sarcasm. "Don't let her make you think you're the punchline."

Something about the way he said it—dry, protective—made Van laugh, small but real. Colby grinned, a flash of warmth under the sun.

For that one beat of a moment, the noise of the field fell away.

THE SECOND HALF DRAGGED. Missed passes. Fumbled runs. The maroon team found their rhythm, and Heritage unraveled like a thread pulled loose. Van's body ached; each mistake landed like a stone in his chest. His father's voice rose above the rest, a running commentary of disappointment disguised as coaching.

Jeremiah still dazzled—his movements smooth, almost

rehearsed. Daphne shrieked approval from the bleachers, clapping like she'd been born to cheer him on.

Van drifted to the edges again, his form blending with the field, his name forgotten in the noise.

When the final whistle blew—Heritage down by two—the cheers were polite, tired. Jeremiah still clapped him on the shoulder. "We'll get 'em next time. You played tough."

Colby followed, more certain. "You held the line, man. That's no joke. Don't listen to the noise."

The words landed heavy, but they held him steady.

As Van trudged toward the fence, his grandmother's eyes found him from her chair. She didn't wave. She didn't clap. She just gave a single, deliberate nod. The kind that didn't need sound to mean *I saw you.*

Van's throat tightened. That one small gesture was enough to keep him from falling apart completely.

THAT EVENING, the house sank into its familiar quiet. The dishwasher hummed, the walls creaked, and the faint sound of the television leaked from his parents' bedroom.

Van sat at the family computer, the dial-up shriek filling the kitchen until the connection clicked into place. The monitor glowed cold blue against his face. His buddy list blinked to life:

no Jeremiah. no Daphne.

He waited anyway.

Then—**ding.**

ChoirNerd88: *"hey. it's miriam. u played good today. i mean it."*

Van blinked. Miriam—the girl from youth choir, always tucked behind the altos, quiet, unnoticed.

He typed back slowly. *"thanks. i messed up a lot tho."*

A pause. Then her reply appeared, each word careful, unpretentious.

"everyone messes up. but u stopped that big guy in the 1st half. i saw it."

Van leaned back, staring at the glow of her message. Nobody had said it like that—not Coach, not Jeremiah, not even his grandmother. Her words weren't loud, but they settled deep, warm and still.

He didn't type again. He just let the message stay there, pulsing faintly in the corner of the screen, filling the room with quiet light.

When the connection finally cut with a hollow click, the house returned to silence.

Outside, crickets thrummed in the dark, steady as a heartbeat.

And for the first time in a long while, Van didn't feel invisible —just *seen,* in the smallest, truest way possible.

AFTER THE WHISTLE

The minivan rattled out of the gravel lot in a long hush, dust curling behind it like smoke from a brushfire. Emmalee swung her legs against the vinyl seat, scuff-scuff, scuff-scuff, humming off-key and clutching the snow cone coupon she'd forgotten to use. Millie twisted the radio dial until a country ballad found its way through static, but the singer's drawl just floated on top of the tight, coiled silence.

At the first stoplight, Jeff spoke without looking back.

"You embarrassed me out there."

Van's water bottle slicked in his hands. He kept his eyes on the night smeared against the window, as if that darkness needed studying.

"You stood like a scarecrow for half the game," Jeff went on, voice flat, practiced. "If Jeremiah hadn't been covering, they'd have doubled the score. That's not what a Shelton puts on a field."

"Jeff—" Millie tried, but he cut her off with a slap of his palm against the steering wheel.

"Don't Jeff me. The boy needs to hear it. Life doesn't hand out medals for breathing."

The words sat heavy in the van. Even Emmalee's humming

folded itself away. Van set his forehead to the glass. The blur of houses and cracked sidewalks slid by, and he imagined the window swallowing him whole—one gulp, and he'd be a quiet smear of light like everything else.

By the time the van nosed into the driveway, the porch light had clicked itself on twice and then settled. Grandma sat on the swing, cane propped beside her, the set of her jaw saying she'd seen enough to fill a ledger.

Inside, roast chicken warmed the kitchen, plates lined up in tidy confidence as if order could tame the day. Van tried to slip down the hall, but Jeff's voice landed like a gavel.

"Sit down."

He lowered into the chair, bag still on his shoulder. Jeff planted himself at the head of the table, arms crossed like a question with only one answer. "One good block and then what? You winded yourself out. You looked weak. Men don't carry themselves like that."

Millie set the roll platter down harder than she meant to; the plate rattled. "He's thirteen, Jeff. Not thirty."

"That's exactly the problem."

The kitchen door creaked. Grandma's cane tapped once, then again, a metronome for truth.

"Jeffrey Shelton," she said, full name landing like scripture. "I sat there and watched your boy throw his whole heart into a block that saved your team. And you? You sat with your arms crossed like Pharaoh himself, too proud to clap for your own flesh and blood."

Silence clanged. Jeff's jaw worked, but nothing came out.

Heat burned behind Van's eyes. Grandma lowered herself beside him, her cool, veined hand covering his. The grip was steady, the kind that says *stay upright; I've got you.*

"You played with courage," she said, softer now. "That's worth more than a scoreboard. Don't forget it."

Millie stood paused over the mashed potatoes, eyes flicking

between her mother-in-law and her son. For a moment, Van saw it—the wish for armor of her own, the kind that spoke truth without apology.

"He needs grit," Jeff muttered at last, but the fight had thinned out of the words.

That night, Van lay in the dark and replayed his grandmother's voice instead of his father's. For once, her words rang louder.

Sunday morning, Heritage Baptist swelled with chatter under the vaults. Halfway through the service, an alto cracked sharp enough to rattle glass. From the row behind, Aunt Sheila leaned forward and breathed, "Mercy, if that's joyful noise, I'd hate to hear the sad one."

Millie covered a laugh with her hymnbook. Van bit his lip.

After the benediction, Mr. Clark, the choir director, waylaid them in the aisle, glasses sliding down his nose. "Van, isn't it? Your Aunt Leslie says you're always humming. Ever think about youth choir?"

Before Van could answer, Jeff said, "He doesn't sing," like it settled the matter.

Mr. Clark smiled past him. "We could use a tenor. Come listen Wednesday. No pressure."

Van's heart tripped. "Okay," he whispered.

On Wednesday he slipped into the back of the loft. The air smelled like hymnals and lemon polish, the scent that clung to every corner of church. Teenagers clutched folders, half-nervous, half-giggling. Mr. Clark pressed music into Van's hands. "Follow along. Sing if you feel like it."

At first his voice was a thread—barely there, tucked under the altos. Then the melody rose and something unlocked. The sound settled in his chest and lifted, warm and unshaken. Mr. Clark's head snapped toward him, eyes bright. "Well, would you listen to that! Shelton, you've got a gift."

Van flushed hot all the way to his ears. But the heat wasn't shame. It felt like pride finding a place to live.

In the hallway afterward, Jeremiah cornered him with a grin. "You sing now?"

"Trying," Van shrugged.

"You weren't trying," Jeremiah laughed. "You were drowning out half the loft. In a good way."

Daphne tittered nearby, a high little chime Van barely heard. For once, the compliment didn't feel like pity. It landed and stayed.

He carried it home like a small, steady flame—pocket-sized, bright, his.

CHAPTER 29

A VOICE THAT WON'T STAY QUIET

The fluorescent lights in the choir room hummed at a pitch that set Van's teeth on edge. The place smelled faintly of pencil shavings, old carpet, and the lemon cleaner the janitor favored on Wednesdays. Teenagers slouched across folding chairs like they'd been poured there, voices ricocheting off cinderblock walls—loud laughs, whisper conspiracies, the occasional squeak of a chair leg dragged just to hear it.

Van sat second row, hymnal quiet in his lap, thumb riding the corrugated edges of the pages. His stomach had been fluttering since last week, when his voice—his voice—had stretched to fill the rafters without cracking. He hadn't meant to be noticed. He wasn't sure it was good. But Mrs. Clark had noticed, and now the flutter felt like a bird who'd realized the window was open.

"Alright, listen up!" Mrs. Clark tapped her pencil against the stand, a crisp rhythm that cut the babble. "Fall revival in two weeks. Youth choir leads. We're doing 'His Eye Is on the Sparrow.' It will stretch you."

A ripple of groans. "That's too high," an alto muttered. Someone else stage-whispered about hiding in the back row.

Mrs. Clark only smiled, eyes bright behind her lenses. "Which is why we'll need a soloist."

The room shifted. Giggles. Elbows to ribs. Van's stomach lurched as her gaze slid down the rows, unhurried, inevitable.

"Van," she said, steady as stone. "I want you to sing it."

The fluorescent hum seemed to grow louder. Van's chest tightened. "M–me?" The word cracked like dry kindling.

"Yes, you," she said, gentle but immovable. "Your tone is clear, your range is steady. God gave you this gift—don't you dare bury it."

Laughter burst from the back. Seth elbowed Colby, mouthing *choir boy*. A pair of girls snorted into their folders.

Colby didn't laugh. His eyes stayed on Van—serious, a little proud.

Two rows ahead, Jeremiah twisted around, grinning like it was the week's best news. "Dude, that's awesome."

Heat crawled up Van's neck. "I—I don't think I can—"

"You can," Mrs. Clark said, bell-clear. "And you will. This isn't about what you think you can't do. It's about trusting what you were given."

Whispers swelled, but her words cut through and rang.

That night at dinner, the news hit the table with the mashed potatoes. "They've asked Van to sing a solo at revival," Millie said, voice light but trembling at the edges of pride.

Emmalee squealed, clapped until her doll face-planted in gravy. "I'm sitting in the very front!"

Jeff's fork paused midair. "A solo?" The judgment came baked in.

"Yes, Dad," Van said to his peas.

Jeff snorted. "Perfect. Can't run a mile without coughing his lungs up, but he can warble with the ladies. What's next—robes and a tambourine?"

Van's fork slipped, clattered against the plate. Heat flooded his ears.

"Jeffrey Shelton." Grandma's voice cracked across the table, sharper than any hymn. She sat tall, silver hair pinned neat, cane like a scepter by her chair. "I won't sit here while you mock the boy for finding what he's good at. You spent months shouting at him on that field. He finally uncovers a gift God put in him, and your first impulse is to tear it down?"

Jeff's jaw bunched. He chose silence.

Grandma turned to Van, eyes softening. "Don't you let anyone —anyone—shame you out of what makes you shine. Not even your own daddy."

Millie's hands stilled on the serving spoon. For a heartbeat, Van saw a flare of longing in her face, like she wished someone had said the same to her once.

By Sunday, word had traveled faster than gossip. Aunt Leslie cornered him in the foyer, cooing *precious* until he wanted to crawl under the welcome table. Aunt Sheila just smirked behind sunglasses. "So the quiet one's getting the spotlight." Then, lower, only for him: "Don't let 'em make a circus of it, baby. Sing it for yourself. Sing it for the One who gave it."

Rehearsals tightened like a drum. Mrs. Clark worked him verse by verse until his ribs ached from breathing. "Lift it, Van. Let it carry. Don't hide."

Every crack raised heat in his neck; every missed pitch tasted like failure. But then the note would find its rung on the ladder— clean, strong—and light would spill in his chest like stained glass waking.

Jeremiah clapped loudest when it landed. "That's it, Shelton!"

Daphne perched near the piano, curls bouncing, smile sugared. "Careful, Jeremiah," she sang out once. "Your best friend's stealing all your thunder."

The laughter was quick, cheap. Jeremiah chuckled, shoulders loose, but Van saw the flicker in his eyes before the grin clicked back into place—unease he kept stapled down.

Van stuffed his folder into his bag, throat tight. Colby slid close and murmured, "Don't listen to her. You were good. Really good."

Not loud. Not showy. But it steadied him more than the applause.

That night, after a dinner that curdled into sharp words and Grandma's fierce defense, Van crept to the family computer. The screen's glow turned the dining room into a small aquarium.

Buddy List

Sportz4u2nv — Online

Soccrallstar — Away ("Soccer 24/7. Hit me up")

ding

> Sportz4u2nv: heard about the solo. dude, that's awesome.

> Treblemaker16: idk if i can do it.

> Sportz4u2nv: u can. you always surprise ppl. even yourself.

The cursor blinked. Van typed *thanks*, sent it, and logged off before he could over-explain the way he always did.

In bed, he whispered the opening line into the dark. His own voice startled him—clearer than he expected, braver than he felt. He pressed his face into the pillow and said it again.

For the first time, the sound didn't feel like something to hide.

It felt like something he could carry.

CHAPTER 30

ECHOES BEFORE REVIVAL

The posters went up first—bold red on thin white paper, taped crooked to every door that mattered at Heritage. **FALL REVIVAL — A TIME TO BE RENEWED.** The paper puckered where condensation from the water fountain licked the corners; a strip of Scotch tape curled like a question mark above the fellowship hall sign. Someone had drawn a halo over the word *Revival* in bright highlighter, its yellow glow bleeding across the serif letters like cheap stained glass.

Beneath it, smaller type: *Youth Choir Leading Worship.* And there, in black pen on the program draft Mrs. Clark kept tucked inside her music folder: **SOLO — "His Eye Is on the Sparrow" (Van Shelton).** Every time Van saw his name, his stomach tilted like a carnival ride that fooled you with a slow start and then dropped you anyway. The flip never lasted. It settled lower each time, but it never left.

Wednesday nights grew electric. The choir room thrummed with fluorescent hum and pencil taps, with teenagers sliding into chairs like they were arriving late to themselves. Mrs. Clark stood at the music stand, spine straight as a metronome, tapping a sharpened No. 2 against the metal lip. "Energy!" she barked, but it didn't feel scolding. It felt like she was winding a key inside the room. "Sing like the Spirit's already fallen, not like you're dragging through clay."

Van stood front and center now—no back row to hide in, no alto tide to cover a falter. The first note wobbled some nights, a thin thread trying to remember what it was attached to. But when it lifted—when his lungs remembered the measure and the sound found its rung—the room changed. Heads lifted. Eyes flicked toward him. Even the humming lights seemed to lean in.

It terrified him. It thrilled him. It made him want to run and stay in the same breath.

Jeremiah always clapped first, loud and unembarrassed, grin splitting open like summer. "That's my boy, Shelton!" he'd call, palms stinging the air until others followed.

Daphne's sweetness arrived a beat later, the burr that comes with the peach. "Careful, Jeremiah," she sang out once, curls bouncing as she reclined against the piano. "He's showing you up. Guess you're not the golden boy anymore."

Laughter sparked too fast, as if her tone had lit dry grass. Jeremiah chuckled with them, shoulders loose, but Van saw the muscle jump along his jaw before the grin locked back in place. Van lowered his gaze to the black forest of notes, waiting for the staves to stop shimmering.

After rehearsal, the gym swelled with the usual migration: basketballs thudding like a second heartbeat, soda tabs cracking open, gossip moving like weather across the polished floor. Daphne orbited Jeremiah on autopilot—palming his sleeve, tipping her head so her braid brushed his shoulder, glancing sidewise to see who was watching her watch him. The act didn't look practiced; it looked like she'd never known another way to be.

"So," she trilled, "you sitting with me during revival? They say the preacher saves the best altar call for the last night."

"Jeremiah and Daphne—revival romance!" Seth whooped

from the bleachers, pounding a beat on the metal seat until it sang.

The circle cracked open with laughter. Jeremiah rolled his eyes, grin easy as a tossed ball. Van still caught the small flinch—the way the grin had to be set, like a hymnbook someone kept straightening.

Colby drifted to Van's shoulder, his presence quiet the way steady things are. "She's like a mosquito," he muttered, low enough to be only for them. "All buzz, no brains." His elbow found Van's, a nudge that said *don't let her rent space in your head.*

Van exhaled. The knot under his sternum loosened one notch. Colby didn't say much, but what he said had weight.

At home, revival talk steamed up the kitchen like a pot left on low. Millie wrote dates in the wall calendar—loops and careful points, her script the domestic twin of a ledger. Emmalee paraded the hallway with her doll as congregant, singing slivers of *This Little Light* to an audience that could not clap. The house smelled of dish soap and lemon cleaner and whatever you call the scent of a family trying not to fight.

Jeff barely looked up from the paper. "He better not embarrass us," he said to the classifieds, not the room. "Everyone'll be watching."

"He won't," Grandma answered, seated regally at the end of the table with her cane leaning like punctuation. Her voice didn't raise; it settled. "And if they are watching, maybe it's time they saw more than you give him credit for."

The newsprint stilled. Jeff's jaw worked like a stuck hinge. Van kept his face turned toward the counter, heat rising in his cheeks like he'd been caught stealing pride.

Sunday brought the soft thunder of shoes on tile and the bright noise of perfume under vaulted wood. After service, the vestibule filled with hugs and programs and the choreography of small-town holiness. Near the organ, Mrs. Clark caught Van's sleeve. "Remember," she said, eyes bright behind shining lenses, "revival isn't about impressing anyone. Let the gift do its work. Trust it."

He nodded, throat tight. *Trust it* sounded like advice and a dare at once.

In the flow of the crowd, Jeremiah's palm found Van's back. "Two weeks," he said, warm and certain. "You're going to crush it."

From across the foyer, Daphne's voice floated like perfume that overstayed. "We'll see if the little sparrow can really sing."

Van flushed, the old impulse to shrink already tugging at his shoulders, but Colby's voice cut clean behind her: "Better a sparrow than a crow."

A ripple of laughter rolled in the opposite direction for once. Daphne's smile faltered half a beat—small, but Van saw it and kept the knowledge like a lucky penny.

The days tunneled forward, each one rimmed in rehearsal. Mrs. Clark worked him measure by measure, her pencil tapping time against the stand. "Lift it, Van. Don't muscle it. Let it ride the breath; let the breath ride the note. Don't hide." Sometimes his voice buckled and shame rushed in like a draft through a bad seal. But then—then the note would land where it should, clean and unforced, and light would break inside his chest as if the room had a new window.

Jeremiah clapped too much and too loud, which should have embarrassed both of them but didn't. Daphne kept up her running commentary—sugar with an aftertaste. "Careful, Jeremi-ah," she cooed once, "your best friend's stealing all your thunder." The room laughed in reflex. Jeremiah laughed too, then pressed his lips together like he'd remembered something too late.

Van packed his music fast that night, paper edges cutting his fingers, but Colby sidled in and bumped his shoulder again. "You were good. Really good," he said, simple as tap water. It landed deeper than applause.

At home, the posters in his mind stuck themselves to the

backs of his eyelids. He lay awake and whispered the opening line, barely enough sound to disturb the dark. His own voice surprised him—clearer than he felt, braver than he planned. He said it again. The second time, it felt less like a noise he made and more like something he let through.

In the mornings, his father still left for work early and came home braced. In the afternoons, Millie still hummed while she stirred a pot. In the evenings, Grandma still read her Bible like correspondence. The world went on mostly the same. The change lived under the skin—quiet as a pulse, insistent as one too.

Two weeks stretched out like a taut string—one you could hear if you put your ear close. Revival posters taped crooked to doors. Programs with his name in black ink. A music folder with soft corners and penciled breath marks. Boys who joked too loud. A girl with teeth wrapped in sugar. A friend whose hands always knew where to steady.

And under all of it—through the gym noise, the kitchen steam, the fluorescent hum—ran a single, stubborn line of melody.

A voice inside him that, for once, refused to stay small.

CHAPTER 31

REVIVAL NIGHTS

The sanctuary of Heritage Baptist had never looked so swollen with bodies or expectation. Folding chairs had been dragged in from every Sunday school room, crammed into aisles until the fire exits felt more suggestion than rule. Fans mounted to the high plaster ceiling whirred in endless rotation, stirring the July air without cooling it. The scent of starch and powder clung to every sleeve, mingling with perfume, sweat, and the ghost of casserole that still haunted the fellowship hall.

It was revival week, and in Fayetteville that meant no excuses. Attendance was duty, enthusiasm proof of salvation. Pastor Rich had said it three times from the pulpit the week before: *"The Lord can't renew what doesn't show up."* So everyone showed up—pressed and polished, hymnals clutched like passports to heaven, their faces lit with the polite strain of people trying to look transformed.

Van slid into the pew between Emmalee and his grandmother. His sister swung her patent-leather shoes against the wood rhythmically, her doll in matching lace resting on her lap. Grandma had insisted on coming—had declared it, really. "No sense hearing about my grandson secondhand." And once

Grandma decided something, heaven and earth adjusted around it.

She looked almost regal in the heat. Her silver hair was coiled into a bun so precise it seemed carved, her lipstick a defiant rose against the soft pastels around her. The carved cane beside her pew gleamed like polished mahogany, and the deacons—grown men in pressed suits—still stepped aside when she passed.

"Sit up straighter, Donovan," she murmured now, giving his elbow a small, authoritative nudge. "The choir's about to come in. You'll thank me when the photographers take pictures." Van straightened at once. No one defied Grandma Shelton.

The youth choir filed in from the side doors, robes rustling like slow thunder. Jeremiah was easy to spot—his blond hair combed within an inch of order, his grin wide and certain. A row of girls in the front pew squealed softly at his glance, fanning themselves with programs. Daphne was there too, curls shining like polished brass, waving across the pews as if she'd just stepped onstage. Colby and Seth shuffled behind them, robes wrinkled, cracking jokes under their breath about who'd hidden candy in the hymnals.

Van kept his eyes on the floor until a firm hand touched his shoulder. "Donovan." Mr. Clark, the choir director, leaned down, glasses slipping to the end of his nose. His tone was calm but deliberate, the kind of voice that didn't ask—it appointed. "I've heard you singing with the congregation," he said. "Tonight, I want you to step out."

Van blinked up at him. "Step out?"

"Solo," Mr. Clark said, already turning away, climbing the steps toward the loft before Van could protest.

The word landed heavy as stone. *Solo.*

The sanctuary swam for a second. All he could see were faces —rows and rows of them. His father three pews back, arms crossed, expression unreadable. His mother smoothing Emmalee's hair like it might keep her hands from trembling. The noise of the crowd pressing in—fans, coughs, rustling paper—all of it closing over him.

Grandma leaned in, voice low but unyielding. "You don't sing for them, Donovan. You sing for the Lord. And don't you dare look at your father's face while you do it."

He blinked, throat tight, the words catching on the edge of his breath.

"You've got this," she said, eyes glinting like glass in candlelight.

The service rolled forward on the rails of routine—hymns, handshakes, testimonies that dragged too long. But Van barely heard any of it. His palms were damp against the varnished pew. Every word from the pulpit sounded muffled, as if spoken through cotton. When the youth choir stood, his knees nearly buckled. The risers looked higher than he remembered, a gallows wrapped in sheet music.

The lights above glared hot and holy. The crowd was a blur of pastel faces and shining foreheads. Jeremiah caught his eye across the row and flashed him a quick grin—like they were teammates again, like this was just another field and another kind of game. Van tried to swallow the panic, to breathe past the knot in his throat.

The piano began. The choir swelled behind him, their voices lifting like the first gust of a summer storm. Mr. Clark's hand rose, the cue sharp and sure. Van stepped forward.

The first note trembled, a ghost of sound barely big enough to reach the microphone. Then another breath—deeper, surer. The melody caught. The room hushed. Every fear, every echo of *"men don't sing"* and *"don't embarrass me"* faded into the soft hum of organ keys. He wasn't singing for them. Not for his father, not even for Grandma's fierce pride. He sang because the sound had been waiting too long to be let out.

When the final note drifted through the rafters, there was a heartbeat of silence—then applause. Polite at first, then swelling, warm, unplanned. Jeremiah whooped once, sharp and bright. Grandma didn't clap; she just nodded once, proud and satisfied, as if she'd known this would happen all along. From the back pew, even Jeff Shelton's hands moved—two stiff claps that echoed louder in Van's memory than they ever did in the room.

The fellowship hall buzzed like a hive cracked open. Crockpots lined the counter, casseroles steaming beside bowls of banana pudding. Perfume, barbecue, and gossip wove together into a haze. Deacons congratulated one another for "a good turnout," while the youth choir laughed, already shedding their robes for T-shirts and sneakers. Jeremiah clapped Van on the back, still grinning. "You killed it, Shelton. I told you, man— you've got pipes." Van smiled, awkward and quiet, but something inside him glowed like an ember that wouldn't go out.

Daphne swept by, curls bouncing, voice sweet as syrup. "Well, looks like our little sparrow found his wings." Jeremiah chuckled. "Told you he'd surprise everyone." Daphne's laugh faltered. Van saw it—and, for once, didn't look away.

The house was silent later, save for the creak of settling boards and the hum of the refrigerator. Van sat at the family computer in the corner of the den, the glow of the screen painting his face pale blue. The modem's dial-up shriek filled the dark until the connection clicked and held. His buddy list blinked to life.

Sportz4u2nv – Away ("Revival. back l8r")
Soccrallstar – Online
A message popped up almost immediately.

Soccrallstar: u killed it 2nite. legit chills.

Treblemaker16: felt like i was gonna throw up.

Soccrallstar: lol well u didn't. u made em clap.
even ur dad.

Van stared at the screen. *Even your dad.* The words pulsed like a metronome, truer somehow in pixel and type than they'd felt in the sanctuary. He leaned back in the chair, headphones around his neck, the faint ring of applause still echoing in his chest.

For the first time, he didn't feel invisible. Just seen. And maybe—just maybe—heard.

CHAPTER 32

A VOICE UNCOVERED

The first verse blurred past in a haze of heat and harmony, the youth choir's sound folding together into one bright, practiced swell. Van mouthed the words without sound, praying Mr. Clark had forgotten. Maybe that quick command—*"Step out"*—had been meant for someone else. Maybe this was all some awful mistake.

But then the instruments thinned. The piano softened to a hush. And from the corner of his vision, Mr. Clark's hand lifted—direct, certain—pointing straight at him.

Van's chest seized. For a single, paralyzing heartbeat, no sound came at all. Then—air. Sound.

It was thin at first, trembling on the edge of breath. But the note held. Clear. Steady. Not perfect, but real. Higher than he thought he could reach, yet unbroken.

The sanctuary shifted around him. Heads turned. Conversations stopped mid-whisper. Someone gasped, too loudly—*"That's Van Shelton?"*

The second line came easier, carried by something deeper than courage—a pull, a release. Fear didn't vanish; it changed shape. It became motion. It became sound. The voice that left his throat wasn't small anymore. It filled the rafters and slipped through the stained glass, finding its own space in the heat-heavy air.

By the time he reached the end of the verse, Van dared to look up.

His grandmother was already on her feet, clapping before the music had even finished, her rose-colored lipstick curved into something fierce and proud. His mother sat beside her, still as stone, tears shining at the corners of her eyes as one hand pressed to her lips. Emmalee bounced up and down in the pew, pigtails flying, shrieking, "That's my brother!" loud enough to startle half the row.

And his father—arms crossed, jaw tight—was clapping. Not joyously, not freely, but still clapping. Like the eyes on him had left no other option. Like approval had to be forced into existence.

The choir surged into the chorus, voices merging again. But Van's no longer vanished beneath them. His wove through, strong and unhidden, riding the final line all the way to the rafters.

When the last note hung there—weightless, suspended—the sanctuary erupted. Applause. Shouts. A scattered "Amen!" from the back row. For once, the sound wasn't pity or politeness. It was something else entirely.

Van stood frozen in it, chest heaving, face flushed. He didn't know whether to laugh or cry.

After the service, the fellowship hall was a storm of casserole dishes, laughter, and perfume. The youth swarmed him before he could find an exit. Hands clapped his shoulders; someone tousled his hair. "Didn't know you had pipes like that!" Seth bellowed, nearly dropping a plate of banana pudding.

Colby's praise came quieter, more certain. "You were good, Van. Really good."

Jeremiah's grin was wide, his eyes bright with pride. "Guess we've got ourselves a secret weapon now." The words were teasing, but his tone—his gaze—made them ring true.

Van smiled, dizzy with it all, until Daphne drifted in like smoke.

She hooked an arm through Jeremiah's, her laugh practiced and sharp. "You sounded good too," she said sweetly, though Jeremiah hadn't sung a single note outside the chorus. The group laughed. Jeremiah laughed, too—half real, half something else. The shift was subtle but familiar: the moment when joy got smaller, when the air around him bent toward someone else.

The circle tilted, leaving Van at the edge. The noise grew, all chatter and movement and perfume, until it pressed against his ribs. He slipped away toward the hallway, breath shallow, searching for quiet.

That's where his grandmother found him.

"You were magnificent," she said simply, her cane tapping the tile before she reached out to cup his cheek. Her hand was cool, her eyes steady. "Don't you let anyone steal that from you—not even family."

His throat caught. "Thanks, Grandma."

His mother appeared a moment later, a napkin crumpled in her hand, eyes still glistening. She looked between the two of them, her voice small but sincere. "I wish I had your way with words," she murmured to her mother-in-law.

Grandma's fingers tightened lightly on Van's shoulder. "Sometimes words aren't needed," she said. "Sometimes just seeing someone for who they are—that's enough."

For a moment, the three of them stood together in the middle of the noise—grandmother, mother, son—a fragile circle of belonging holding its ground in the storm of chatter and casseroles and congratulations.

Later, when the house fell silent and only the hum of the refrigerator kept time, Van sat in the dim kitchen with the computer glow washing his face.

Sportz4u2nv: *Online.*
Soccrallstar: *Away — "Homework. Be back."*
The message blinked alive:

> Sportz4u2nv: u seriously killed it.

> Treblemaker16: nah. just got lucky.

> Sportz4u2nv: not luck. u have a voice. ppl saw it.
> i saw it.

Van's chest tightened. His throat burned. He typed back slowly: "thanks." The word looked too small, but it was all he had.

A moment later, Jeremiah's away message flickered back on: *"Hanging w/ friends. Don't page me."* The screen dimmed, the kitchen light buzzed, and the silence grew large again. But Van didn't log off. He sat there, letting the hum of the monitor fill the room like an echo of his own heartbeat.

Upstairs, he lay awake long after the rest of the house went still. The echo of his song drifted through the dark—clean, steady, still alive.

Not shame. Not fear.

Something closer to wonder.

For the first time, he felt proud—of something that was his. Not earned through someone else's approval. Not measured against a whistle or a shout. Just his. Real. Unborrowed.

Something that could grow.

CHAPTER 33

FINDING HIS VOICE

The weeks blurred like watercolors left out in the rain—edges smudging, colors bleeding until one day melted into the next.

Van woke each morning to the shriek of his alarm clock, the kind of sound that tore through dreams like a blade through cloth. He'd smack it into silence, drag himself upright, and shuffle through the motions of another day.

By night, he collapsed again, still half-dressed, mind spinning with words he hadn't said and notes he hadn't quite hit.

School. Choir. Soccer. Church. Repeat.

The rhythm never changed—only the masks did.

Student. Teammate. Son. Maybe-soloist.

He lived in the seams where they overlapped, stretching himself thin to fit each version expected of him. Between algebra tests and drills, hymnals and homework, he tried to hold the line —afraid that if he slipped, the whole version of himself he was pretending to be might unravel.

CHOIR AND SOCCER divided him cleanly.

One demanded grace.

The other, grit.

The choir room smelled like floor wax and graphite, the sharp metallic scent of old music stands. Mrs. Whitaker's baton carved the air, her voice crisp and unyielding.

"Float, Shelton. Don't muscle it."

He tried. His chest expanded, air trembling behind his ribs. The note wavered once, then found itself—clearer than he meant it to be.

A hush rippled through the rows. Even Seth, who spent most rehearsals crossing his eyes behind the altos, muttered, "Dang, Shelton."

From the second row, Miriam Carson's voice broke the silence.

"You sounded like a Disney prince," she blurted. Then, realizing what she'd said, flushed crimson. "In a good way! Not corny —just… strong but shiny."

Laughter rippled. Seth snickered, but Miriam held her ground, pushing her glasses up the bridge of her nose.

"I mean it," she said, quieter now. "You sounded amazing."

The word hit him like a slow echo.

Amazing.

No one had ever used that word for him before.

When rehearsal ended, she lingered near the door, fingers fidgeting with the strap of her backpack.

"You're lucky," she said softly. "To have a voice that makes people stop talking. I'd kill for that."

Van shrugged. "Guess I just got lucky."

Her gaze didn't waver. "No," she said. "You just don't believe it yet."

The words lodged somewhere deep, unsettling in their honesty. They followed him long after the last bell rang.

. . .

THE SOCCER FIELD told a different story.

No harmony. No patience. Only sweat, shouts, and the sting of failure.

"Plant and push, Shelton!" Coach Thomas's voice cracked across the field.

Van gritted his teeth, feet digging into the dirt. He shoved against the forward's charge, forcing him wide of the goal.

"Better," the coach barked, already looking away.

From the fence, Jeff Shelton gave a single, brief nod.

It wasn't praise, not really—but it wasn't nothing either.

By the end of practice, the field lights burned halos into the dusk. The team sprawled in the grass, all noise and laughter—Seth's bad jokes, Brandon's arguments about fries, Colby's quiet chuckles that always made the chaos seem manageable.

Jeremiah sat a little apart, Daphne tucked too close beside him, her lip gloss catching every bit of light.

"A pastor's son needs a pastor's daughter," someone teased.

Jeremiah laughed, but it rang hollow. Van saw the tension behind it—the tiny crack in the performance.

Still, the whispers spun, relentless as gnats.

On the ride home, Van slouched in the back seat, head against the cool window. Colby sat beside him, one earbud dangling.

"You did good today," Colby said. "Didn't let that guy through once."

Van managed a tired grin. "Thanks."

Colby shrugged, turning the volume down. "My dad noticed. Jeremiah too. He just… didn't say it."

The words lingered, heavy with what they didn't say.

Didn't say it echoed louder than impressed.

SATURDAY'S CHOIR rehearsal stretched long into evening. The air was thick with the smell of dust and eraser shavings, the hum of the vending machine filling every pause. Chairs scraped, voices faded, and Van stayed behind to stack hymnals.

"You're going to do great on that solo," Miriam said from the doorway.

He laughed under his breath. "You've got too much faith in me."

"No," she said, steady this time. "You don't have enough in yourself."

It wasn't scolding. It wasn't pity. It was a truth she handed him like something fragile but meant to last.

He nodded, unsure what else to do.

Outside, the September evening hummed with cicadas and the faint whistle of a train far down the tracks. The parking lot lights threw long, uneven shadows, stretching the edges of the night.

Van stood there a while, feeling the weight of the week fade under the noise of the world around him.

Colby's quiet encouragement.

Miriam's certainty.

Coach's reluctant praise.

Even his father's single nod.

Each thread pulled tight inside him, weaving something small but certain—a sound taking root that was neither forced nor borrowed.

For the first time, Van didn't hate the sound of it.

For the first time, he didn't want to hide it.

THAT NIGHT, the computer hummed in the corner of the kitchen, its screen casting pale light across the countertops. The dial-up tone shrieked, then clicked into silence.

His buddy list blinked alive.

xXChurchChicXx has signed on.

ChoirNerd88: Online.

JereDavis11: Away — *Homework. AIM me l8r.*
Sportz4u2nv: Online.
ding

> ChoirNerd88: heard whitaker gave u the Pie Jesu
> solo. that's huge.

> Treblemaker16: pretty sure i'll choke.

> ChoirNerd88: no way. u'll make ppl cry. in a
> good way.

The cursor blinked at him, waiting.

Van leaned back, watching the glow paint his reflection in the dark window. His heart thudded with something warm, unsteady.

ding

> Sportz4u2nv: heard the same. u got this.

> Treblemaker16: we'll see. i still sound like i
> swallowed sand.

> Sportz4u2nv: nah. u sound real. that's why ppl
> listen.

A pause. Then another message appeared, slower.

> Sportz4u2nv: don't let anyone talk u out of it. not
> even u.

Van's fingers hovered over the keys. He typed, erased, typed again. Finally:

> Treblemaker16: thanks. guess we'll see if the
> sparrow can sing again.

Jeremiah's away message flipped back on: *Out w/ friends. Don't page me.*

The chat dimmed, the cursor blinking like a heartbeat.

Van didn't sign off right away. He just sat there, the house quiet except for the low hum of the refrigerator and the faint ring still in his ears—the sound of his own voice refusing to disappear.

He closed his eyes.

For the first time, the noise in his head didn't feel like chaos.

It felt like music.

And it was his.

By the time September bled into October, the echo of that summer solo had faded from the rafters, but its weight still lingered—soft as dust, heavy as truth.

CHAPTER 34

THE BALANCING ACT

By the time September bled into October, the sound of his own voice no longer felt foreign.

But balance—balance was another matter.

The first week of sophomore year hit like a wave that didn't care who it dragged under. One moment, summer had stretched wide and golden—revival nights humming with hymns and heat, soccer fields steaming beneath the July sun, the echo of Van's solo still carrying faintly through the days like a secret he was afraid to speak aloud. The next, it was gone—swallowed by early alarms, crowded hallways, and the sour-sweet smell of pencil shavings, floor wax, and cafeteria coffee.

High school moved fast, a blur of sneakers and gossip, slammed lockers and laughter that never quite belonged to him. Van moved through it in a quiet rhythm of survival: get to class, keep your head down, don't draw attention.

Daphne, on the other hand, thrived in it. She was everywhere —bright and deliberate, like a parade that refused to end. Her curls bounced as she glided between lockers, her binder covered in doodled hearts and Bible verses written in thick pink marker. "Proverbs 31" looped across the front like a brand. She carried her faith like a banner, loud and polished, and her presence followed Jeremiah through every hallway like perfume.

She caught Van off guard one afternoon outside the choir room.

"You know," she began, voice tilted with mock curiosity, "for someone who acted all shy, you've got people talking."

Van blinked, shifting his backpack higher on his shoulder. "What do you mean?"

"That solo." She smiled—sharp, almost kind, but never quite. "You crushed it." She leaned closer, lowering her voice as if sharing a secret. "Honestly, I didn't think you had it in you. Guess you were hiding that voice on purpose."

Van fumbled for something to say, heat rising to his neck. "I just didn't want to sound awful."

"Well, you didn't," Daphne said briskly, already half turned toward the sound of Jeremiah's laughter echoing down the hall. Her tone changed instantly—lighter, higher, dripping with delight. "Jeremiah!" she called, waving as he passed with a grin and a handful of teammates.

Van stood there, the echo of her earlier words—you crushed it—folding in on itself until pride and emptiness sat tangled in his chest.

Choir rehearsals and soccer drills carved up his week like two competing sermons. Algebra homework, youth group on Wednesdays, games on Saturdays, Sunday services that stretched into the night—it was a life packed so tight it squeaked. He tried to hold all the pieces without dropping any of them, terrified that if he let one slip, the rest would scatter too.

By Friday, the balance started to buckle.

He stumbled off the soccer field drenched in sweat, his jersey clinging to his back, lungs clawing for air. He'd missed an easy block, Coach Thomas barked until his whistle nearly cracked, Colby tried to joke it off, and Jeremiah—again—was somewhere orbiting Daphne's laughter. The sound of it carried across the field, bright and distant, and stung worse than the sunburn striping Van's neck.

By the time he got home, his body felt hollowed out. The front door creaked open into the smell of spaghetti and lemon cleaner. The TV murmured low in the next room. He'd just pulled off his cleats when his father's voice came from the recliner.

"Donovan. A word."

Van froze, heart thudding. Slowly, he padded into the living room. Jeff Shelton sat half-lit by the glow of the muted television, his face carved with lines of work and worry. For once, his expression wasn't hard—just tired. The kind of tired that came from years of pushing everything forward, no matter who got caught behind.

"Sit," he said.

Van obeyed, bracing for another lecture about grit or focus or falling short.

But Jeff didn't raise his voice. He leaned back instead, arms crossed loosely, eyes fixed somewhere beyond the screen. "You sang real well the other night."

The words landed like a stone in still water—soft, then rippling.

Van blinked. "Thanks."

Jeff nodded slowly. "I know I don't say much about choir. Not my world. Couldn't carry a tune in a bucket. My old man—your granddad—used to say singing was for women and preachers. Waste of time for a real man." He let out a humorless chuckle. "Guess that stuck in my head more than I realized."

Van sat still, afraid to breathe too loud.

Jeff rubbed the back of his neck, voice quieter now. "I know I've been hard on you. Soccer, school, church—those make sense to me. Music?" He paused. "That's different. And when I don't know how to help, I guess it comes out like I don't care."

His eyes finally lifted, meeting Van's. "But I do. I'm proud of you. You've got something that's yours. Something you're good at."

Van's throat tightened. He wanted to say thank you, but the word felt too small, too breakable. "Thanks, Dad," he whispered anyway.

Jeff exhaled through his nose, a sound somewhere between relief and surrender. "Don't think this means you get to slack on soccer," he said, a faint grin tugging at his mouth. "But… maybe I'll try to listen more. Even if I don't understand it."

It wasn't an apology, not really. But it was more than Van had ever gotten.

A door cracked open. A light that didn't flicker out right away.

Later, lying in bed, the ceiling fan hummed a low rhythm above him. The house was still, the walls breathing softly with summer heat. He replayed his father's words—quiet, clumsy, real —and somewhere underneath them, his grandmother's voice echoed like a steady drumbeat: *Don't you let anyone steal that from you—not even family.*

Van turned toward the window, where moonlight cut a pale line across his desk, and smiled faintly.

For the first time, the balance didn't feel impossible.

Just fragile.

But real.

By the following week, the rhythm had settled again—school, soccer, choir, repeat. But beneath the noise and motion, something else had begun to hum quietly in him. A pulse. A voice that refused to fade back into the background.

CHAPTER 35

VOICES CARRY

esday's sky sagged the color of notebook paper smudged with pencil. By last period, the gym had shed its basketball lines and bleachers for rows of folding chairs, scraped into uneven arcs that echoed with every drag. A faded Christmas banner—**GLORIA IN EXCELSIS**—drooped from the far wall, one corner held up by duct tape and habit.

The air hung thick with lemon cleaner, floor wax, and the faint sweetness of the body spray the sopranos swore by. The fluorescent lights hummed overhead—steady, relentless—matching the nerves fluttering in Van's chest.

Mrs. Whitaker stood dead center, baton poised like a weapon. "From the chorus," she ordered, her eyes locking on him. "And you, Shelton—float it. Don't yank it."

A ripple of laughter slid through the bass section. Van's ears burned, but he lifted his chin. The accompanist struck the opening chord—sharp, resonant—and the room folded into hush.

He inhaled until it hurt. The solo line neared. Whitaker's baton lifted—one, two—then stilled midair. His cue.

Van opened his mouth, and the note came like a secret escaping. It wasn't loud or showy, but pure—thin as thread, strong as wire. For three beats, it hung there, hovering above the gym's scuffed floors and chipped paint. Even the hum of the lights seemed to pause, as if the room itself had leaned closer to listen.

Seth whispered, "Dang, Shelton."

Colby gave a low whistle.

Miriam Carson—blushing behind her glasses—breathed out, "That was amazing."

Van ducked his head, pulse hammering. "Uh…thanks."

Mrs. Whitaker snapped her baton down. "If that's 'fine,' then angels have been lying to us for centuries. Again. Float it this time."

They ran it twice more. Each time, the sound left him easier—less pulled, more given. By the third run, he wasn't forcing the note; it was finding him.

When rehearsal ended, the air felt lighter. Van gathered his folder, hands still trembling faintly. The praise—quiet, awkward, honest—followed him out the door, catching on his sleeves like dust he didn't want to brush away.

THAT NIGHT, the house hummed in its usual pattern—TV murmuring from the next room, the dishwasher sighing through its cycle. Van sat at the kitchen table, the blue light of the computer washing over his hands.

Buddy List — Active:
JereDavis11: Online.
xXChurchChicXx: Away — "Talking 2 someone special ;)"
ChoirNerd88: Online.

ding

ChoirNerd88: still think u sounded amazing.

Treblemaker16: just glad i didn't screw up.

A pause, then:

ChoirNerd88: u didn't. u have a gift.

He stared at the blinking cursor until the words blurred, the glow softening the edges of the room. His throat tightened. He didn't type back this time. Some things felt too big for the smallness of text.

When he finally shut the computer, the silence didn't feel empty. It felt full—like the sound still lived somewhere inside him.

WEDNESDAY NIGHT, the gym was the youth group's again—its order replaced with chaos and Kool-Aid stains. Folding chairs pushed aside. Basketballs thudding. Voices colliding in laughter that rose too fast, too loud.

Daphne sat close beside Jeremiah, her perfume thick and sweet, her voice pitched just right for an audience. "So, you got a Homecoming date yet?" she teased, tilting her head. The circle around them giggled. Jeremiah smiled his easy smile—too smooth, too practiced—but Van saw the flicker in his eyes before he looked away.

Van drifted toward the far hoop with Colby. They took turns missing shots and pretending they didn't care.

"The only rule is we're allowed to suck," Colby said, launching a hopeless brick that hit the rim and clattered off.

Van laughed, real and unguarded, the sound catching him by surprise. "Then I'm already winning."

"Yeah," Colby said, smiling. "Guess you are."

The ball rolled to a stop between them. For a moment, everything—Jeremiah's laughter, Daphne's chatter, the squeak of sneakers on the gym floor—faded into the distance. The world shrank to the space between their breath and the echo of the ball hitting the floor.

Van didn't know what it meant yet, only that it felt easier here.

Simpler.

Honest.

When he left that night, the air outside was cool and damp, carrying the faintest trace of rain. Somewhere between the hum of the streetlights and the sound of his own footsteps, Van realized something quiet and sure:

The voice inside him wasn't just growing.

It was beginning to carry.

CHAPTER 36

EXPECTATIONS

Saturday morning came crowned in dew. Chalk lines glared white against the grass, coaches' whistles split the air, and parents unfurled lawn chairs like battle flags. Someone's grill hissed in the distance—charcoal smoke curling above the parking lot, too early for hot dogs, right on time for nerves.

Coach Thomas paced the sideline like a preacher at the pulpit. "We're not out here to look pretty," he barked. "We're here to be *present*. Blow a play? Next touch. Don't write poetry about your mistakes."

Jeremiah bounced on his toes, energy coiled in every tendon. Colby rolled his neck, loose and unbothered. Van rotated his ankle until it popped, wishing the sound counted as courage.

The whistle shrieked.

The world collapsed to motion: the slap of cleats, the sting of air in his throat, the thud of the ball against shin guards. He bricked his first clearance—too soft, too slow. Reset. The next came faster, cleaner. He planted hard, angling the forward wide until the shot died harmlessly into the side net.

Coach clapped once. From the fence came his father's voice— gruff but warming. "That's better!"

Midway through the half, Jeremiah carved a seam only he could see. Two touches. A feint. The ball bent past the keeper's glove like it had always known where it belonged. Net.

The fence erupted.

"That's my boy!" Daphne's voice sliced above the others, syrupy and triumphant. Jeremiah brushed her fingers through the chain link—habit, performance, maybe both. The crowd loved it.

Van's gut twisted at the words. *My boy.*

Colby jogged past, murmuring, "Breathe." Just that—simple, steady, enough.

They won—barely—but they won. The team mobbed Jeremiah, spraying water like champagne. Seth stumbled through the chaos, soaked and laughing. Pastor Rich clapped from the sideline, his approval braided tight with expectation.

Jeremiah's grin, for once, was real when he found Van. "Crash at my place tonight? Pizza, FIFA, movies. So I can expose how you button-mash."

Van smirked. "Bold talk for a guy who almost lost us the first half."

Colby passed, giving Van's shoulder a light bump. "Good wall today." Simple words, but they held weight—anchoring him more than the noise ever could.

THAT NIGHT, the Davis house smelled of lemon polish and pizza grease. Pastor Rich greeted Van with a handshake firm enough to count as a lesson. Ms. Denise smiled warmer, pressing a cookie into his hand before he could refuse.

Jeremiah's room was neat in that deliberate way boys clean before company—bed made, posters straightened, clothes shoved out of sight. They sprawled across the carpet, the movie's flicker painting their faces in blue and gold. Wrestling for the last breadstick ended with Jeremiah pinning Van, grinning like they were twelve again.

Laughter came too easy.

Then Jeremiah's phone buzzed. *Daphne.* Again. He flipped it facedown, sighing. "Feels like my schedule got written without me."

Van stared at the ceiling fan, its soft click keeping time. "You could say no."

Jeremiah's half-smile said otherwise. "Can I?"

Later, when the house fell into its quiet rhythm—creaking floors, the low drone of a muted TV—Van lay on a folded quilt, staring into the dark. Pastor Rich's voice drifted faint through the walls: "...he's the pastor's son... people are watching..."

Denise's reply came softer, but sure. "He's still a boy, Rich."

BACK HOME, the computer hummed awake, filling the kitchen with its familiar blue light.

Buddy List — Active:

JereDavis11: Away — "Sleep. Big day 2moro."

xXChurchChicXx: Online.

ColbyKicks17: Online.

ding

ColbyKicks17: solid game today. u held ur line.

Treblemaker16: thanks. u too.

The cursor blinked. Nothing more followed. But those three words—*solid game today*—carried farther than applause, sermons, or Daphne's cheers ever could.

Expectations weren't always shouted. Sometimes they arrived as whispers through walls, as glances over chain-link fences, as AIM messages glowing in the dark.

And sometimes, they steadied him—quietly, invisibly—even through the static of dial-up.

190

"The first time truth trembles inside you, it sounds like music."

CHAPTER 37

THE SOUND OF BECOMING

Sunday morning arrived lacquered in shine.

The Shelton house spun in its usual pre-church chaos—Millie ironing Emmalee's bow for the second time because the first one "looked tired," Emmalee whining about tights that pinched behind her knees, and Jeff checking his watch every few minutes like time itself needed disciplining. Van wrestled with his tie in the hallway mirror, pulling it too tight, then too loose, wishing he could wear anything that didn't feel like a leash.

By the time they piled into the van, tension buzzed like static. Emmalee kicked her shoes against the vinyl seat, humming tunelessly. Millie flipped through her Bible, dog-earing the passages she guessed Pastor Rich would choose. Jeff adjusted the rearview mirror twice, though it was already straight. "We're late," he muttered, even though they weren't.

Heritage Baptist shimmered under the bright morning sun—cars packed in neat rows, families unloading like well-rehearsed stage crews. Fathers tugged jackets into place, mothers herded children with polished smiles, and toddlers wriggled in protest against bows and buckles. It looked less like worship and more like performance—everyone desperate to sparkle just enough to avoid scrutiny.

The foyer smelled of perfume layered over bitter coffee. Greeters beamed at every arrival, hands extended like audition tapes for friendliness. "Blessed morning! So glad to see you!" sang out again and again.

Aunt Leslie stood guard near the bulletin table, voice sweet as syrup. "Millie! Jeff! Oh, Emmalee, don't you look precious." Her gaze landed on Van. "And Donovan—my, how handsome. Growing like a weed."

He mumbled thanks, edging closer to his mother. Compliments from Leslie always came wrapped in measurement.

Inside, sunlight poured through stained glass in fractured color. The sanctuary glowed—polished pews, brass fixtures gleaming. The Sheltons slipped into their usual spot halfway back. Jeff tugged his tie once more; Millie whispered reminders to Emmalee to sit still, fold her hands, behave. Van smoothed the front of his jacket and tried to shrink smaller inside it.

When the choir rose, his pulse quickened. Filing into the loft, he felt the weight of every gaze—Mrs. Whitaker's most of all. Her sharp look caught him and held, unspoken but unmistakable: *Deliver.*

The organ swelled. Voices rose. The sanctuary filled with harmony that pressed against his ribs.

Van mouthed the words, waiting. Then, as the hymn climbed toward its middle, the organ softened. The choir hushed.

It was his turn.

He drew a breath the way Mrs. Whitaker had drilled into him —"from the basement, not the attic." The first note trembled but didn't break. The second steadied. The third opened wide, effortless. His voice lifted through the rafters, threading light through the colored glass. Even the restless toddlers stilled, their small faces tilted toward the sound.

For those few measures, nothing else existed. Not soccer. Not his father's critiques. Not Jeremiah's orbit around Daphne. Only sound—clear, true, wholly his.

When the last note fell, silence lingered, full and reverent. Then applause rose—not polite, but real. It filled the sanctuary like wind rushing through open doors.

Heat rushed to Van's face. His hands trembled as he lowered the hymnal.

Down in the pews, his grandmother stood first—clapping like she was cheering a homecoming win, her eyes wet but shining. Millie pressed a hand to her mouth, blinking fast. Even Jeff, arms crossed and expression tight, gave a single nod. It wasn't much. But it was something.

When Van slid back into his seat in the loft, Colby leaned over with a grin. "Told you," he whispered. "That was solid. Not fake, not forced—just you. Don't let it slip."

The words hit deeper than the applause.

Across the sanctuary, Jeremiah caught his eye and mouthed *I told you so*, his grin wide and proud. Beside him, Daphne clapped delicately, already leaning to whisper something to the girl next to her. But Van hardly noticed.

His chest trembled—not from nerves, but from something gentler. For once, he hadn't hidden. For once, he'd been seen.

THAT AFTERNOON, the Shelton kitchen smelled of fried chicken, mashed potatoes, and his grandmother's biscuits steaming on the table. The meal carried a rare ease—no sharp edges, no simmering arguments, only warmth settling in the spaces between laughter.

"That was a gift, sweetheart," his grandmother declared, laying down her fork. Her voice carried quiet authority, the kind that silenced everyone else. "Don't you ever doubt that. And don't hide it, either. Hiding's just another kind of pride."

Van flushed. "Yes, ma'am."

Jeff cleared his throat, rubbing the back of his neck. "It was…
stronger than I expected. Good work."

Simple words. But from him, they landed heavy and full, like
something he'd been trying to say for years.

His grandmother nodded, satisfied. "That's your boy up
there," she said, turning toward Jeff. "First time he's kicked that
ball straight into that fishing net thing."

The table went quiet.

Jeff pinched the bridge of his nose. "Mama, it's called a choir
loft. He was singing, not—"

"Don't you correct me, Jeffrey Allen Shelton," she cut in, her
eyes narrowing with the same fire that used to keep him in line as
a boy. "I know what I saw. I saw my grandson win the whole
game."

Millie's laughter burst out before she could stop it. Emmalee
clapped along, delighted. Van ducked his head, smiling into his
plate.

For an hour—between the biscuits, the teasing, and the hum
of pride that filled the room—the air in the Shelton house felt
lighter than it had in years.

And for the first time, Van didn't just have a voice.

He had a home for it.

CHAPTER 38

LINES IN THE SAND

*A*fter the evening service, Heritage Baptist's gym changed skins again—its polished floor shedding the quiet reverence of hymns for the rattle and echo of sneakers. Folding chairs screeched against waxed wood, and laughter scattered like marbles. It was Youth Afterglow night—half fellowship, half frenzy, and the one time of the month when the teens could linger in God's house without the sharp gaze of parents or pastors cutting through the noise.

The air was its own perfume: Kool-Aid, lemon cleaner, cheap frosting, and the faint musk of sweat buried under the scent of sugar. The snack table sagged beneath trays of store-bought cookies and neon cupcakes. Two sweating jugs of cherry punch glistened in the fluorescent light, leaking condensation into sticky puddles.

Van stood near the wall, Styrofoam cup in hand, watching the chaos unfold like a spectator to someone else's dream. The room had already organized itself into familiar constellations—the loud kids orbiting the center, the quiet ones in their small corners, and the awkward in-betweeners floating like lost satellites. He took a sip of Kool-Aid; it tasted like syrup and childhood, staining his tongue red.

Jeremiah was in his usual place—magnetic, effortless, his presence bending the room toward him. Even standing still, leaning casually against the snack table, he drew gravity. Daphne clung to his arm, laughter spilling in bright, practiced bursts. Her nails brushed his sleeve with intention, the gesture rehearsed. Possession disguised as affection. She was staking claim on stage and making sure everyone had a front-row seat.

Van didn't want to watch. But his eyes betrayed him again and again, tracing Jeremiah's grin—the kind that didn't reach his eyes, the tension in his shoulders when Daphne leaned in too close.

Colby's voice arrived beside him, steady and unexpected.

"Looks like a play."

Van blinked. "What?"

Colby nodded toward the center of the room. "Them. Jeremiah and Daphne. All that laughing, all that glow—it's staged. Like they're trying to sell tickets." He shrugged, easy, eyes never leaving the scene. "I don't buy it."

Van forced a laugh. "Everybody else does."

Colby's voice softened. "Everybody else wants to."

For a moment, the words hung there—half observation, half mercy. Then Colby glanced sideways, his mouth curving faintly. "By the way, you played good defense this week. Better than I've seen."

Van looked over, startled. "Thanks," he said, and the warmth behind the word caught him off guard.

Colby nodded. "Coach noticed. So did Jeremiah. He didn't say it, but… he saw it."

The comment landed deep, like a steady hand pressing between his shoulder blades. Van didn't answer, afraid his voice might crack under the weight of something that felt too rare to name.

Then Seth crashed in, frosting smeared across his chin.

"Breaking news!" he shouted, mock announcer voice booming. "Jeremiah and Daphne have been declared Heritage Baptist's golden couple. The youth group has spoken!"

Colby didn't even look over. "Blessings on their union," he said dryly, swiping a cookie from Seth's plate and handing it to Van. "You look like you need this more than him."

Van laughed, surprised at how easily it came. "Thanks."

Colby grinned. "Don't thank me. Thank his terrible reflexes."

The gym buzzed around them—volleyballs thudding, shrieks from a collapsing human pyramid, the rattle of laughter from every corner. Pastor Rich's voice floated faintly from the doorway, half a warning, half surrender: *Not above head level, please!*

Van and Colby lingered near the wall, companions in the quiet part of the noise. Sometimes they talked—about drills, fries, Mrs. Whitaker's baton. Sometimes they didn't. The silence between them didn't itch. It just breathed.

Eventually, parents began calling names, the noise dissolving into coats and farewells. Millie appeared with Emmalee in tow, her bow crooked, cheeks stained pink from sugar. His father muttered about traffic, ushering them toward the exit.

Across the lot, Colby's voice called, "See you Tuesday!" He raised two fingers in a lazy salute before slipping into his dad's truck. For a moment, his hand lingered on the glass—a wave half-finished, half-felt.

In the minivan, Van leaned his forehead against the window, the cold humming through his skin. The gym's lights glowed faintly in the dark, halos dissolving in the night air.

He exhaled, the glass fogging, then clearing. The image of Jeremiah and Daphne lingered sharp in his chest. But Colby's grin—quiet, unhurried, unclaiming—echoed somewhere deeper.

Two truths, side by side. Two lines, drawn in the same sand.

And for the first time, Van wondered if one of them finally led somewhere he belonged.

SHIFTING GROUND

Tuesday's sky stretched thin and colorless, half gray, half blue—like it couldn't decide whether to lift or fall. By the time Van trudged through the double doors of Piedmont Valley High, the hum of fluorescent lights overhead felt crueler than sunlight. The hallways pulsed with the usual symphony: lockers slamming, sneakers squeaking, voices rising in gossip and laughter.

Everything smelled faintly of cafeteria grease and pencil shavings—a mix that made it hard to breathe.

His backpack felt too heavy. Not with books, but with everything else—choir, soccer, youth group, Jeremiah's shadow, Daphne's perfume, Colby's words still playing softly in the back of his mind.

By last period, the gym had transformed again into its second identity: choir rehearsal hall. Folding chairs fanned out across the floor, and Mrs. Whitaker stood like a queen with her baton as her scepter. "Let's lift it up, loves. Float, don't drag."

Miriam sat one row ahead, nervously fidgeting with her pencil. She turned when Van dropped his music folder onto the seat beside her.

"Hey," she blurted, cheeks already pink. "Your solo the other day—it was amazing. Like, I didn't know you could sing like that."

Van ducked his head, heat prickling up his neck. "Thanks."

"No, really," she said, earnest now. "Most people sound scared when they go high, like you can *hear* them bracing for disaster. But you didn't. You just… made it sound easy."

Seth snickered from behind them. "Dang, Shelton, didn't know you had groupies."

The sopranos giggled. Miriam froze, mortified. Van wanted to disappear.

"Less chatter," Mrs. Whitaker snapped. "From measure thirty-two. Tenors, silk thread, not rope. Shelton—float."

Van exhaled, whispering, "Silk thread. Got it."

The accompanist struck a chord. The room hushed. His voice rose, light and clear, steadying midair like it belonged there. Even Seth leaned forward. When the final note faded, Miriam clapped once before remembering herself.

"Told you," she whispered.

After rehearsal, Van lingered to stack chairs. Miriam hesitated nearby, shifting her books from arm to arm.

"So… uh, Homecoming?" she blurted. "Are you—going?"

He blinked. "Probably not."

"Oh." Her smile faltered. "Right. I just thought—never mind." She fled before he could find words, leaving a strange guilt heavy in his chest.

That evening, the field glistened from an earlier drizzle. Coach Thomas's whistle split the air. "Plant, Shelton! Don't fall on me now!"

Van gritted his teeth, braced, and pushed through the tackle. The ball skidded wide.

"Better," Coach barked.

His father's voice carried from the fence. "That's it! About time!"

Half praise. Half dagger. But it still landed.

Across the field, Jeremiah gleamed—every move crisp, every laugh too bright. Daphne cheered like she'd been rehearsing all week. "That's my boy!"

Van looked away. He didn't need the reminder.

Colby jogged up beside him, tossing a water bottle his way. "You held that line better tonight," he said. "Didn't let Brandon past you once."

Van blinked. "Thanks."

"Coach saw it. Jeremiah too," Colby said, resting his hands on his knees. "He just doesn't always say it."

Something inside Van settled. The whistle blew again, sharp and insistent, but Colby's words stuck with him longer than the drill.

That night, lying in bed, the ceiling fan hummed above him like a steady metronome.

He thought of four faces—Miriam's blush, Daphne's grin, Jeremiah's brightness, Colby's quiet. Four different pulls, each tugging at some part of him he didn't yet know how to name.

The world around him kept shifting, but one thing was certain: the ground beneath him was no longer still.

CHAPTER 40

OFF KEY

Thursday's light slanted through the tall windows of the gym-turned-choir-room, dusty gold cutting through the stale air. Folding chairs gleamed faintly beneath the fluorescents, and the faint smell of lemon cleaner and floor wax still lingered from morning P.E.

By the time Van slipped into his usual seat, the place already hummed—shuffling music folders, sneakers squeaking, and the low murmur of teenagers not yet ready to focus.

Mrs. Whitaker stood at the front like a conductor carved from steel and lace, her baton flashing like a warning.

"Altos, from measure twenty-eight," she called, then flicked her gaze toward the tenor row. "And tenors—eyes up, shoulders open. Mr. Shelton, that means you. I can *hear* when you get lazy."

Heat crept up Van's neck. He straightened his folder, pretending to study the notes even though he knew them by heart. His voice wasn't off—it just wasn't steady. Not today. His mind was a carousel of noise: Jeremiah and Daphne, the last game, Colby's quiet encouragement still echoing under his skin.

Mrs. Whitaker tapped the stand again. "Breathe through it,

don't fight it. The note wants to live; you just have to get out of its way."

The accompanist struck the chord. Van inhaled, the paper-soft scent of sheet music mixing with sweat and floor polish. He opened his mouth, and the sound came—not perfect, but clean enough to make her baton pause midair.

A small nod. That was all he got. But from her, that was everything.

When rehearsal ended, the clatter of chairs filled the air like applause for the wrong show. Voices overlapped—laughter, teasing, the slam of music stands. Van was halfway to the door when Miriam appeared beside him, clutching her folder like a shield.

"Hey," she said, slightly breathless, pushing her glasses up with her wrist. "You sounded really good again. Like… scary good."

Van smiled faintly, rubbing the back of his neck. "Thanks."

"No, I mean it," she said quickly. "You're probably the best tenor we've had in years. Mrs. Whitaker practically worships your vocal cords."

He laughed under his breath, shaking his head. "I doubt that."

Miriam's sneakers squeaked as she shifted her weight. "So, uh… Homecoming's coming up. Are you—"

Before she could finish, Seth's voice sliced through the noise from across the gym.

"Hey, Van! Quit flirting with your girlfriend and help me with these stands!"

The laughter that followed hit like a slap. Miriam went crimson. Van's stomach dropped. "She's not—" he started, his voice cracking worse than his high note last week.

Seth just grinned wider. "Oh, come on. Don't act like she doesn't have heart-eyes every time you sing."

A few altos snorted. The sopranos tried to hide their giggles behind sheet music. Van groaned, grabbed his folder, and stomped toward the stands. "Shut up, Seth."

Behind him, Miriam muttered a soft "See you tomorrow," and ducked out before he could find the words to make it right.

THAT NIGHT, the world traded melody for mud.

The soccer field was slick from a drizzle that hadn't committed to rain. Floodlights glared against the mist, turning everything silver. Coach Thomas's whistle cut the air like a blade.

"Dig in, boys! You're not playing for your moms—you're playing to win! Jeremiah, lead that charge! Shelton, for the love of —plant your feet!"

Van gritted his teeth, driving his cleats into the soaked turf. The forward lunged; Van held. The ball deflected wide, and Coach barked, "Better!" in a tone that could've meant a dozen things.

Then, from the fence line—his father's voice.

"That's it! About time!"

The words stung, even dressed in praise. Always *about time*, never *good job*.

Van shoved the feeling down and focused on breathing, on running, on anything that wasn't the ache sitting under his ribs.

At the far end, Jeremiah was a blur of precision and grace, every motion effortless, every goal expected. Daphne's voice cut through the chill air:

"That's my boy!"

Van heard it, like everyone else.

He didn't look.

He didn't need to.

He tied his bag too tightly, pretending the knot needed adjusting. His pulse still beat to that same impossible rhythm—too loud, too fast, always behind.

Colby jogged up beside him, breath visible in the damp. "You're holding the line better," he said, tone easy.

Van looked up, surprised. "Yeah?"

"Yeah," Colby said. "Coach saw it. Jeremiah too. He just…" His eyes flicked toward the fence. "…doesn't always say it."

Van swallowed. "Figures."

Colby bumped his shoulder lightly. "You don't need them to say it for it to be true."

For a moment, everything went quiet—the noise of the team, the cheer from the bleachers, even the sting of his father's voice. All that remained was that small, grounding truth, steady as breath.

BACK HOME, Emmalee chattered in the minivan's back seat about her spelling test, her voice bright as tinsel. His parents spoke in clipped, tired tones.

Van pressed his forehead to the window, the glass cool against his skin, and watched the field lights fade into the dark.

The world kept spinning fast around him—expectations, noise, belonging—but something in him was starting to slow down, to listen.

And in that quiet, he began to realize that maybe being *off key* wasn't always being *wrong*.

CHAPTER 41

ECHOES BETWEEN US

By the time October settled in, Heritage Baptist had two different heartbeats.

One belonged to the church—the fall festival flyers, the chili cook-off sign-up sheet, the hollow promise of "fellowship through fun."

The other belonged to the school—soccer playoffs, Homecoming chatter, hallways humming with gossip.

Van existed in the middle, straddling both worlds, belonging fully to neither.

Choir rehearsals stretched longer under Mrs. Whitaker's baton. "Perfection isn't impossible," she declared, eyes like searchlights. "It's just inconvenient."

Coach Thomas said the same thing in a different language. "Effort is everything. Leave it all on the field."

And his father said nothing at all, which somehow said the most.

Meanwhile, Jeremiah and Daphne had become the youth group's unofficial poster couple. She was at every game, every event, every practice she could crash—her cheers syrup-sweet and loud enough to drown out anyone else's.

He smiled through it, always smiling.

And everyone around them nodded like the story made perfect sense.

Van tried not to care.

But caring was second nature.

SATURDAY'S MATCH played under a sky that smelled like frost. The air had that brittle edge that warned of winter coming fast. Parents lined the fence wrapped in blankets and scarves, the sound of clapping muffled by gloves.

Jeremiah scored once—a perfect arc that sliced through the air like light. The bleachers erupted, Daphne's voice loudest of all:

"That's my boy!"

Van didn't flinch this time.

He just anchored himself, eyes on the field, waiting for the next rush.

When it came, he was ready.

Plant. Push. Don't give ground.

The forward broke right—Van blocked. Another charge, another hold. The ball died on the line, swallowed by the grass.

Coach Thomas clapped once. "Good defense, Shelton."

From the fence, his father's voice followed: "That's better, Donovan!"

It wasn't praise so much as permission to stop proving himself for a heartbeat.

He'd take it.

By the end of the game, they'd tied—half victory, half loss—but Van's pulse still thrummed like triumph. Jeremiah was swarmed at the fence, Daphne wrapping herself around him like a spotlight.

Van sat on the bench, untying his cleats, pretending to focus on knots instead of the ache that twisted deeper.

Colby dropped beside him, tossing a water bottle between his palms. "Good stops today," he said.

Van laughed softly. "You think so?"

"I know so," Colby replied, bumping his shoulder. "Coach knows too. And your dad—well, that's about as close to love as his tone gets."

Van barked out a laugh, startled by how much lighter it felt to share that truth.

Colby grinned. "See? Getting there."

The floodlights buzzed overhead. Their shadows stretched long across the grass—two figures sitting side by side, quiet in a world that always demanded noise.

THAT NIGHT, the gym glittered with sagging paper pumpkins and orange streamers curling from the basketball hoops. The Youth Afterglow was in full swing again—cookies, Kool-Aid, chaos.

Jeremiah was the center of it all, Daphne perched beside him like a crown she never took off. Everyone watched them, smiled at them, built stories about them.

Van stood by the bleachers, Styrofoam cup in hand, watching without wanting to. The sweetness of the drink coated his tongue until he couldn't taste anything else.

"Not your scene?" Colby's voice came from beside him, low and wry.

Van turned, half smiling. "Is it that obvious?"

Colby shrugged, leaning back against the bleachers. "Only to someone else avoiding the crowd."

They watched in silence—Jeremiah's grin too perfect, Daphne's laughter too sharp.

"Feels like a play," Van murmured.

Colby nodded. "It is. But not everyone knows their lines yet."

Van huffed out a laugh, and the sound felt like relief.

Colby reached over as Van nearly dropped his cup, steadying

it with a quick touch. His hand brushed Van's for a second—small, unremarkable, but charged with something that made Van's throat go dry.

They stayed there for most of the night—talking sometimes, saying nothing other times. When Colby joked about the crooked pumpkin decorations ("That one looks like it's witnessed unspeakable crimes"), Van laughed so hard he spilled Kool-Aid on his sleeve.

And for the first time, the noise around him didn't feel like something he had to survive. It just… existed, and so did he.

As the night thinned out and parents began calling names, Colby's dad waved from the parking lot.

"See you Tuesday," Colby called, lifting two fingers in a lazy salute. The grin that followed was quiet but sure—an anchor in motion.

Van climbed into the minivan, the windows fogged from breath and autumn chill. Emmalee sang softly in the back seat, Millie murmured thanks to another parent, and his father muttered about traffic.

But all Van could think of was the space between noise and stillness—the echo that lingered when truth brushed close but didn't need to shout.

Jeremiah's life looked perfect from the outside.

Colby's life felt *true* in the quiet.

And somewhere in the middle, Van realized maybe the place between the two wasn't emptiness at all.

Maybe it was where his own voice was beginning to live.

CHAPTER 42

SHIFTING GRAVITY

Monday mornings at Piedmont Valley always felt like punishment for whatever joy dared to exist over the weekend. The halls buzzed with leftover gossip from Friday's game, Saturday's hangouts, and Sunday's sermons—stitched together into a quilt of teenage noise: who liked who, who bombed the quiz, who got caught sneaking out. The scent of floor wax and cafeteria grease lingered beneath it all.

Van moved through the crowd with his backpack dragging like an anchor, the weight of textbooks thudding against his spine. His legs still ached from Saturday's match, calves tight, a bruise blossoming violet on his shin where a forward had clipped him. He wasn't limping, exactly, but he felt the pull in every step —a reminder that nothing in his world stayed still for long.

At his locker, voices swirled around him in bursts of sugar-coated chatter.

"Daphne and Jeremiah are basically official now," a choir girl gushed, her voice pitched to carry. "Didn't you see her post? She tagged him with a heart emoji!"

Her friend squealed like she'd just heard breaking news. "Pastor's son and pastor's daughter—it's perfect."

213

The words landed like grit in Van's chest. *Pastor's son.* The phrase clung to Jeremiah like a costume he hadn't asked to wear. No one seemed to notice how heavy it looked on him.

Van shoved a notebook into his bag too hard. The locker door rattled shut louder than he meant it to.

"Hey," came Colby's voice—steady, low, familiar.

He leaned against the locker beside Van's, hoodie half-zipped, hair sticking up like he'd lost the fight with his pillow. "You hear the math quiz got moved to Wednesday? Grace of God right there."

Van blinked, then laughed, the knot in his chest easing. "Seriously? I didn't even study."

Colby grinned, eyes glinting. "See? Miracles still happen."

The exchange was small, quick—but it loosened something that had been wound too tight. Colby had a way of doing that. He didn't fix things; he just *shifted* them, like tilting a mirror so the light hit differently.

Choir rehearsal after school carried a different kind of pressure.

The gym-turned-choir-room smelled faintly of floor polish and brass polish, old risers echoing every movement. Mrs. Whitaker stood at the front like a general in pearls, tapping her baton against the stand.

"Pie Jesu from the top," she said crisply. Her gaze flicked to Van. "Remember, Shelton—don't climb the note. Float it. Imagine a feather."

He inhaled, slow and steady, the air tasting like dust and tension. When he sang, the sound left him clean and unforced, rising like breath escaping glass. It filled the space, bounced off the rafters, lingered. Even Seth stopped smirking long enough to glance over.

When the phrase ended, the gym held a brief silence—just long enough for Van to feel it: the strange rush of being heard.

"Not bad, Shelton," Seth muttered finally. "Didn't even sound like you were dying."

Van rolled his eyes, cheeks warming. "Thanks, I think."

From the front row, Miriam Carson looked up from her folder. Her glasses caught the light, her eyes soft behind them. She gave him a small, awkward smile—part admiration, part something else. The paper in her hands crinkled where she gripped it too tightly.

Van blinked, unsure what to do with the attention. He looked away, pretending to adjust his pages.

During break, Colby drifted closer from the baritone section. "You realize she's into you, right?" he said under his breath, amusement curling in his voice.

Van nearly dropped his folder. "What? No. She's just being nice."

Colby's eyebrow lifted. "Sure. Let's call it that."

Van groaned. "Shut up."

"Hey, I'm not judging," Colby said, smirking. "Just observing."

Van laughed despite himself, the sound low and surprised. When the bell rang, it felt less like an ending and more like a reprieve.

WEDNESDAY NIGHT BROUGHT the usual storm: youth group in the church gym, folding chairs in a lopsided circle, Kool-Aid stains already ghosting the waxed floor.

Pastor Rich's devotional on "peer pressure" landed with the soft irony of a sermon no one planned to apply. Then came free time, and the gym dissolved into chaos—basketballs flying, sneakers squealing, laughter spilling into echoes.

Jeremiah was immediately swarmed, as always. Daphne clung

to his arm, laughing at every line of whatever story he was telling Seth. Her voice—bright, sugar-sharp—carved through the noise.

Van and Colby retreated to the far side of the court, starting a game of half-court basketball that neither of them had the coordination for. They missed more shots than they made, but it didn't matter. Their laughter drowned out the scoreboard that didn't exist.

Colby bricked a layup and groaned. "The only rule here is we're allowed to suck."

Van laughed so hard he missed the rebound. "Then we're champions."

Across the gym, Jeremiah sank a basket, and the crowd—mostly girls—erupted. Daphne clapped the loudest, her voice echoing like a cheer routine.

Colby watched the scene, tossing the ball lazily. "Man," he muttered, "it's like watching a highlight reel no one asked for."

Van snorted, almost choking on his water. "Stop."

"I'm just saying," Colby continued, grinning. "Everyone's acting like he's already married. You'd think the church bulletin would print it under 'prayer requests.'"

Van's laughter came loud, too loud, but he didn't care. For a moment, the weight in his chest lifted clean off.

LATER THAT NIGHT, the van hummed along the dark highway, headlights stretching thin across the road.

Emmalee chattered in the backseat about cloud shapes and snacks. His father grumbled about traffic; Millie offered quiet shushing between sighs. Van leaned against the window, his reflection ghosted over the passing streetlights.

Jeremiah's world was tightening—Daphne, the church, the expectations pulling him like gravity he couldn't escape.

But Colby's presence felt different. Quieter.

It didn't pull; it steadied. It didn't demand; it stayed.

Van exhaled, his breath fogging the glass, and traced a small circle in the condensation with his fingertip.

No one else saw it.

But he did.

And for the first time, he wondered what it might mean if that gravity kept pulling.

CHAPTER 43

THE OFFICIAL STORY (POLISHED REWRITE)

*B*y Friday, Piedmont Valley buzzed with a single headline, whispered down locker rows and cafeteria tables like it was breaking national news:

Jeremiah Davis and Daphne Miller were officially together.

It hadn't come from Jeremiah—of course not. He wasn't the announcing type. But Daphne was. Her Myspace post said it all: a Sonic photo, the two of them side by side in the flat glow of a parking lot light. His arm was barely around her shoulder—polite, not possessive—but the caption sealed it:

Game days are better with my guy.

The hearts poured in.

The comments rolled fast.

Cutest couple!

Finally!!

Pastor's son + pastor's daughter = perfection!

By second period, everyone had seen it. Seth cornered Van at his locker, grinning like he'd discovered treasure.

"Check it out," he said, shoving his phone forward. "The pastor's golden boy is officially off the market."

Van stared longer than he meant to. Jeremiah's smile wasn't fake, exactly, but it wasn't the easy grin Van knew either. It was the practiced one—the one he used when adults were watching.

The one that said, *Don't worry, I'm playing the part.*

"That's cool," Van muttered, handing the phone back faster than necessary.

Seth smirked. "Bet Daphne's already picked their wedding colors."

"Probably," Van said, trying to laugh, but it came out thin. His stomach twisted anyway.

LUNCH WAS WORSE.

The cafeteria smelled like pizza boats, milk cartons, and fryer oil that had seen too many Fridays. The noise rolled through in waves—chairs scraping, trays clattering, the hum of teenage gossip.

"She's basically the First Lady of Heritage now," one girl said between giggles.

"Yeah, she'll be leading women's Bible study before she can even drive," another added.

At the center of it all sat Jeremiah, Daphne perched beside him like a jewel everyone wanted to look at. Her laugh was bright and deliberate. Every time he spoke, she tilted her head, eyes locked on him as though he'd hung the moon himself.

Van pushed his food around his tray, appetite gone.

Then Colby dropped onto the bench across from him, tray loaded with fries. He chewed in silence for a beat, then glanced toward Jeremiah and Daphne before leaning forward.

"You'd think the school board was about to issue a press release," he muttered.

Van choked on his milk. "Stop."

"What? I'm just saying." Colby's grin was half a smirk, half salvation. "The way people are acting, you'd think he cured cancer instead of getting a girlfriend."

Van huffed a laugh despite himself. "You're gonna get yourself killed if Daphne hears you."

"Eh." Colby shrugged. "Worth it."

For the rest of lunch, he kept it up—quiet jokes, subtle jabs, small observations only Van could hear. Each one landed like a life raft, keeping Van afloat in a sea of noise that suddenly felt too sharp, too loud.

THAT NIGHT'S game turned the rumor into a coronation.

The air was cool, almost metallic with autumn, breath turning to fog beneath the stadium lights. Parents lined the fence with thermoses and lawn chairs. The crowd roared as the boys took the field, cleats striking the turf like thunder.

From the sidelines, Daphne's voice carried:

"Go, Jeremiah! That's my boyfriend!"

The word **boyfriend** cracked through the night louder than the ref's whistle. The girls beside her squealed, clapping like it was scripture come to life.

Jeremiah didn't flinch. He lifted a hand in acknowledgment, smile automatic, posture perfect.

Van, standing at defense, felt it like a stone to the ribs.

The game blurred into motion: shouts, tackles, the sting of cold air in his lungs, the rhythm of sprint and reset. Twice he blocked clean shots, Coach Thomas barking a rare "Good work, Shelton!" across the field. Each word struck like lightning—brief, bright, gone too fast.

When Jeremiah scored, the crowd detonated. Daphne's cheer cut through it all: "That's my *boy!*"

The team mobbed him, laughter and slaps on the back.

"Boyfriend of the year!" someone yelled.

Van tugged at his jersey, sweat rolling between his shoulders, trying not to watch.

Trying harder not to *feel*.

AFTER THE GAME, steam rose off the field in soft ribbons. The boys sprawled on benches, gulping water, their laughter echoing under the lights. Jeremiah stood surrounded—Daphne clinging to his arm like an accessory she couldn't misplace, teammates orbiting close with teasing grins.

Van sat apart, unlacing his cleats slowly, methodically. The chill bit at his damp socks.

Colby dropped beside him, close enough that their shoulders nearly brushed. He handed over a water bottle without a word.

"Nice saves tonight," he said finally. "Especially that last one."

Van blinked, surprised. "Thanks."

Colby leaned back, watching the commotion around Jeremiah. His voice was quieter now. "They're all acting like he can't breathe without applause." He paused. "I think he hates it."

Van frowned. "You think so?"

"I *know* so." Colby's eyes stayed fixed ahead. "You just gotta watch."

The words settled between them like steady ground—quiet, certain, unshowy.

Van didn't reply. He didn't need to.

For a long moment, they just sat there in the glow of the stadium lights—the noise dimming around them, the cold air humming, something unspoken growing roots between the silences.

LATER, in the backseat of the van, Van pressed his forehead to the cool window. The road slid by in streaks of gold and dark. Emmalee hummed to herself in the back. His father's voice muttered about traffic, Millie's about leftovers, both fading into the rhythm of tires against asphalt.

Out there—beyond the blur of headlights—Jeremiah was already claimed.

His orbit, his image, his every move belonged to someone else now.

But Colby—

Colby's presence didn't demand. It *grounded*.

And while no one else seemed to notice the difference,

Van did.

He could feel it pulling—quiet, certain, impossible to ignore.

"Some forces don't ask permission to pull."

CHAPTER 44

THE PULL

By mid-October, Daphne had become as much a fixture at soccer games as the floodlights themselves.

If Jeremiah was on the field, she was at the fence—her curls bouncing with every cheer, her voice carrying above the crowd like a megaphone wrapped in sugar.

"Go, *babe!*" she called during warm-ups, loud enough for half the parents to smirk behind their travel mugs.

The word *babe* clung to the air longer than it should have. It wasn't new anymore—she'd been saying it for weeks—but each time it hit Van's ears, it landed differently. Not just gossip now. Not rumor.

Official.

At youth group, she sat beside Jeremiah, legs crossed neatly, notebook open but mostly filled with doodles of hearts and swirls.

At school, she waited by his locker, brushing imaginary lint from his sleeve, laughing a little too loudly at jokes Van knew weren't even funny.

And Jeremiah... played along. His hand rested where it should. His smile appeared when expected.

But Van saw the edges—how his shoulders stiffened just slightly, how his laugh rose half a pitch too high, how his gaze drifted to the far wall when no one was looking.

Van noticed because he couldn't not. He'd spent too long watching Jeremiah not to recognize the moments when the performance cracked.

THAT WEDNESDAY, after youth group, the gym echoed with the slap of basketballs and the sugary scent of Kool-Aid. Folding chairs scraped, sneakers squeaked, and laughter bounced off the cinder-block walls.

Van lingered near the bleachers, pretending to retie a shoe that was already tight.

"You're hiding," Colby said, voice low but amused, settling beside him on the step.

"I'm not hiding," Van muttered.

Colby's grin was soft, knowing. "You're sitting on the far side of the gym, tying the same shoe for five minutes."

Van snorted. "So maybe I'm hiding a little."

Colby leaned back on his elbows, eyes following Van's line of sight. Out on the court, Jeremiah played two-on-two, sweat shining on his forehead. Daphne perched nearby, clapping theatrically every time he scored, her laughter slicing through the noise like glitter on glass. The circle around them glowed with attention.

Colby tilted his head, casual. "You can't live in someone else's spotlight, Shelton. Bad for your skin."

Van laughed despite himself. "What does that even mean?"

"It means," Colby said, nudging his knee lightly against Van's, "some of us are better off in the shadows. Less pressure there."

A beat. A smirk. "Better company too."

The words landed heavier than Van expected. He looked at

Colby, but Colby was already watching the court again, his face unreadable except for that faint, steady half-smile.

Saturday's game was brutal.

The opposing team moved like they were built from muscle memory and momentum, their passes sharp enough to slice through air. Van's legs burned, his lungs raw from cold breath and effort. Twice he was shoved hard enough to stumble, but each time he reset—planted, braced, held his ground.

Jeremiah scored once—of course he did—but it wasn't enough. The whistle's final shriek cut through the field like a warning siren: 2–0, them.

Coach Thomas barked about grit, about learning from mistakes. Parents packed folding chairs in stiff silence.

Daphne swept across the grass, curls bouncing, wrapping herself around Jeremiah like the loss hadn't happened at all.

"You were amazing," she said, loud enough for everyone to hear. "It wasn't your fault."

The words carved the field in two.

Jeremiah—and then everyone else.

Van tugged at his socks, staring at the damp blades of grass. The sting of the score settled somewhere behind his ribs.

Colby appeared beside him, voice steady, grounding. "You played solid today. Those blocks in the first half? Saved us from being embarrassed."

Van looked up. "Really?"

Colby nodded. "Really. Coach saw it. I saw it. You held the line."

The way he said it—plain, unshowy, real—soothed something Van hadn't realized was raw.

Colby didn't slap him on the back or toss an empty "good job." He said it like it mattered. Like Van mattered.

. . .

THAT NIGHT, lying in bed, the day replayed in quiet fragments:

Daphne's voice shouting *babe* across the field.

Jeremiah's smile stretched too thin beneath her hand.

Colby's steady tone by the sidelines—*You held the line.*

It was strange, the way gravity worked.

Jeremiah still pulled at him—he probably always would—but lately, Colby's presence had its own kind of force.

Quieter. Steadier.

A pull that didn't demand attention but offered balance instead.

Van didn't have a name for it. Not yet.

But he could feel it now—how it drew him closer without ever asking.

And somewhere, deep down, he knew:

He was starting to shift.

Starting to see where he truly stood.

CHAPTER 45

THE UNSPOKEN LINE

By late October, Jeremiah and Daphne weren't just together—

they were *expected* to be.

It wasn't gossip anymore.

Not whispers in the back of the youth group or sidelong glances in the hallway.

It was settled law.

Every *babe* Daphne chirped across the gym, every hand she looped through Jeremiah's arm, carried the weight of inevitability.

"The golden couple," Seth declared one afternoon at lunch, gesturing with his half-eaten sandwich like a preacher blessing the congregation. "Pastor's son and the prettiest soprano in the choir? Tell me that's not straight out of a Hallmark movie."

The table erupted in laughter, the kind that rolled easy and collective.

Van forced himself to smile, but it landed thin.

Jeremiah shook his head, a grin still fixed in place. "Cut it out, man."

But Daphne didn't argue.

She leaned her head against his shoulder, curls spilling over his jersey, and said, sweet as frosting, "You're just jealous."

The laughter carried on, light and predictable.

But underneath it, something inside Van pressed tight.

It wasn't that Jeremiah had *chosen* Daphne.

It was that it no longer felt like a choice at all.

The church approved. The youth group cheered. The school followed suit.

Jeremiah wasn't dating a girl—he was fulfilling a prophecy.

And no one seemed to see how his smile sometimes flickered the second people looked away.

No one but Van.

FRIDAY NIGHT'S game ended in another narrow loss, the kind that felt like holding your breath too long.

Parents still clapped like it was a victory.

Coolers snapped shut, folding chairs clattered, and the air smelled of sweat, grass, and the ghost of hope.

Daphne waved Jeremiah over from the fence, her bracelets chiming.

"You were the best out there," she said loudly, looping her arms around him for a hug that was half celebration, half announcement.

"Seriously—you carried the whole game!"

Van stood a few yards away, tugging at the velcro of his shin guards, pretending to focus on the mud crusted along the seams.

Her words stung more than the loss.

You carried the whole game.

It wasn't true. Jeremiah had scored, yes—but Van had stopped three drives that should've buried them.

He wasn't asking for credit. He just hated watching truth rewritten in real time.

Colby wandered over, hair damp with sweat, water bottle swinging loosely from one hand.

He followed Van's gaze toward Jeremiah and Daphne, then back again.

"They don't see it," he said quietly.

Van frowned. "What?"

Colby shrugged, voice even. "They don't see how much you hold the line.

They don't see how he leans on you out there.

But I do."

Van let out a small, uncertain laugh. "Yeah, right. Me and my three blocks."

Colby didn't smile. "Three blocks that kept us in the game."

His tone was calm, certain. "Don't sell yourself short, Shelton. You're better than you think."

Van glanced up. For once, Colby wasn't looking away.

Their eyes met—steady, unflinching—and something unspoken sparked in the space between.

Not loud. Not dramatic. Just… *there.*

A flicker of understanding that neither of them named.

For one suspended moment, it felt like Colby was about to say something else—something larger, something dangerous.

Van's chest tightened.

But before he could breathe, Seth jogged past, shouting about pizza, and the spell broke.

Colby looked away, tossing his empty bottle into the recycling bin with more force than necessary.

"Anyway," he muttered, rougher now, "good game."

"Yeah," Van managed. "You too."

THAT NIGHT, the house was quiet except for the hum of the ceiling fan and the tick of the clock down the hall.

Van lay on his back, staring at the faint pattern of headlights moving across the ceiling.

He replayed the look in Colby's eyes, the weight in his voice.

He told himself it was just encouragement—a teammate being decent.

That's all.

But his pulse didn't agree.

Because deep down, he knew it had been more than that.

Outside, autumn pressed its cool breath against the window.

Somewhere, Daphne was still texting Jeremiah hearts and Bible verses.

Somewhere, the "golden couple" shone beneath the church lights.

But here—in this still, quiet space—Van couldn't stop thinking about the smaller light beside him.

The kind that didn't demand attention.

The kind that felt truer simply because it didn't need to be seen.

CHAPTER 46

UNDER THE SAME SKY

Saturday nights had their own rhythm.

The buzz of a game fading.

The drone of his father's voice filling the van on the way home—mutters about missed tackles, about focus, about grit.

The thud of cleats tossed at his feet, the smell of sweat and grass still clinging to him.

Usually, Van would slip away after, let the house quiet around him, and sink into the comfort of being alone.

But tonight was different.

After practice, Colby had leaned in, voice low—steady the way it always was when he said something that mattered.

"Hey," he'd said. "You wanna crash at my place after the game?"

Simple words. But they lit something.

Colby didn't hand out invitations lightly. His circle was wide —he laughed with teammates, traded sarcasm with Seth, nodded at upperclassmen in the halls—but sleepovers were rare. His home felt like a threshold people didn't often cross.

For Van, being asked felt like being chosen.

At home, his mother just smiled when he asked.

"Be polite," she said, brushing his hair back like she used to when he was little.

His father grunted something about not staying up all night like fools, but even that couldn't dim the flicker in Van's chest.

COLBY'S HOUSE sat quiet on a cul-de-sac, porch light glowing soft amber against the autumn dark. Inside, it smelled faintly of detergent and cinnamon—like clean laundry and something warm cooling on the counter.

His room was down the hall, a space that somehow *was* Colby: a little messy, a little confident, familiar.

The dresser held a buzzing tube TV, its screen flickering blues and whites from a late-night action movie.

Posters crowded the walls—wrestlers mid-roar, football stars frozen in victory poses, corners curling where the tape had given up.

A pair of dumbbells sat beside the closet, scuffed with use.

The bedspread was simple navy, but the mattress sagged in the middle, the kind of imperfection that made it human.

Colby kicked off his shoes and dropped onto the bed cross-legged, wearing a fitted T-shirt that clung to his shoulders.

He looked effortless in his own skin—broad, solid, the kind of strength that seemed to hum quietly rather than shout.

Van, still wiry and unsure of his body, couldn't help but notice the difference.

Colby's frame looked like it had arrived exactly on time.

Van's still felt like it was running late.

He unrolled his sleeping bag on the carpet, the zipper snagging on a thread. His hands fumbled like they'd forgotten how to work.

"Movie okay?" Colby asked, nodding toward the screen.

"Yeah," Van said, even though he hadn't caught a single frame of it.

· · ·

THE ROOM GLOWED blue in the TV's light.

Outside, wind whispered against the window screens, the faint sound of a dog barking somewhere down the street.

They talked about nothing—about plays from the game, about Seth's terrible aim with Gatorade bottles, about Mrs. Whitaker's death glare whenever someone missed tempo.

They tossed popcorn until it littered the floor.

And then, somewhere between the jokes and the silence, the air changed.

It wasn't awkward—just *quieter.*

Softer.

The kind of quiet that made every sound feel bigger.

Colby leaned back on one arm, the shifting light cutting across his jaw.

"You know," he said, voice low, "you don't give yourself enough credit."

Van looked up. "What?"

Colby's gaze didn't waver. "You're good. On the field. In choir. You act like people don't notice you, but they do."

He paused, then added, even softer: "I do."

The words landed like a pulse.

Van's throat went dry. His heartbeat tripped over itself. "Thanks," he managed, though it came out almost a whisper.

Colby studied him for a second—then moved.

Not sudden, just deliberate.

He leaned in slowly, his expression unreadable but his eyes sure.

And then, before Van could even think—

their lips met.

A spark—sharp, clean, undeniable.

Van froze, not out of fear, but because everything in him *stilled.*

The world folded down to that single point of contact—the hum of the TV, the warmth of Colby's breath, the faint taste of salt and popcorn and something new.

Colby kissed him again, firmer this time, and the room seemed to tilt.

The air thickened.

The blue glow brushed their faces like water.

When he finally pulled back, Colby didn't laugh.

Didn't apologize.

He just sat there breathing, shoulders rising and falling, his eyes never leaving Van's.

"You're good, Shelton," he murmured, like a confession. "Better than you know."

The words hung there, fragile but full.

Van swallowed hard, his pulse still hammering. He wanted to say something—to name what had just happened—but language had fled.

Colby leaned back into the pillows, exhaling. The faint hum of the movie filled the silence again, as if pretending it hadn't just witnessed something holy.

Van slid into his sleeping bag, inches from the bed.

The glow from the TV reached both of them—same light, same air, the same impossible stillness.

He lay there, eyes tracing the cracks in the ceiling paint, heart still racing beneath his ribs. His lips tingled with memory.

The thought pressed against his mind and refused to leave:

He had spent so long orbiting other people's light—Jeremiah's, Daphne's, even his father's expectations.

But tonight, for the first time, someone had pulled him *into* the light.

And as sleep finally found him, Van realized—

he wasn't just seen.

He was *found*.

"*Silence isn't absence. It's what the heart sounds like when it finally listens.*"

CHAPTER 47

THE QUIET AFTER

Morning came softly, as if the world itself had agreed to keep the secret.

Sunlight slipped through half-closed blinds, cutting the room into stripes of gold and shadow. Dust drifted lazily in the beams, suspended, weightless — the same way Van felt. His sleeping bag was a tangled mess around his legs, the nylon still faintly warm from restless turns. Every beat of his heart replayed the same moment: the lean, the breath, the press of lips, the sudden hush of everything else falling away.

Colby had kissed him.

Even now, hours later, the memory felt too big to hold.

He rolled onto his side. Colby lay sprawled across the bed, one arm thrown over his head, the other resting across his chest. The blanket had slipped to his waist. The faint morning light painted his skin in muted golds and grays, tracing the slope of his shoulders, the curve of his jaw, the rise and fall of each steady breath.

The TV in the corner had gone to static sometime after midnight. It hummed faintly now, a soft, steady pulse that filled the silence between them.

Van swallowed hard, pulling the edge of the sleeping bag closer even though the room was warm. He should have felt panic — shame, maybe, or fear — but instead, there was only the quiet hum beneath his ribs. A thrill that refused to fade.

The bedsprings creaked. Colby stirred, stretching until his back arched, his shirt lifting to reveal a line of muscle that caught the light. His eyes opened, hazy with sleep, and found Van's.

For one heartbeat, neither moved.

Then Colby smiled — small, unguarded. "Morning."

Van's throat tightened. "Morning."

That was all. No nervous laughter, no backpedal, no pretending it hadn't happened. Just the word — soft, simple, enough.

BREAKFAST WAS a different kind of silence. Colby's mother stood at the stove, flipping pancakes that steamed in the chill kitchen air. His little brother argued with the syrup bottle. The radio murmured old country songs beneath it all.

Colby acted normal — maybe *too* normal. He teased his brother about football practice, joked that his mom's pancakes could double as weights. But every so often, his knee brushed Van's under the table, a light, wordless reminder. Each time, the spark returned, small but alive.

When Colby offered more syrup, his eyes caught Van's just long enough for the noise around them to fade.

For the first time, Van felt what it was like to be seen without being paraded. To exist without performing.

LATER THAT MORNING, the world put its mask back on.

Heritage Baptist was a blur of perfume, pressed collars, and voices turned up too high. "Good morning! What a blessing to see you!" echoed like a script everyone knew by heart. The sanctuary gleamed with polished wood and sunlight bleeding through stained glass.

Jeremiah walked in with Daphne on his arm, her curls bouncing, her Bible pressed against his side like a prop. The whispers rose before they even reached their pew.

Such a sweet couple.

Perfect example for the youth.

The pastor must be so proud.

They looked like a photograph — all symmetry and brightness. Jeremiah's smile landed on cue; Daphne's hand clutched his arm with the precision of choreography.

Van sat beside his family, tie too tight, jacket too stiff, his pulse still running to the rhythm of the night before. His father sang the hymns too loudly, his mother mouthed the words, Emmalee dangled her feet against the pew.

Van watched Jeremiah's smile falter in the space between songs — the half-second where performance cracked. No one else saw it. No one ever did.

He looked away, jaw tight.

Because here, under the vaulted ceilings and fluorescent halos, everything was about appearance — the perfect son, the perfect girl, the perfect faith. But Van's world had tilted.

No one in this sanctuary — not Jeremiah, not Daphne, not even his parents — knew what had happened in the blue flicker of that small, quiet room.

No one knew that for the first time, someone had reached for him, *really* reached — not out of expectation or obligation, but because they wanted to.

And as the choir swelled, Van closed his eyes and let the sound rise around him.

The song wasn't the same anymore.

He wasn't the same anymore.

CHAPTER 48

THE QUIET BETWEEN SEASONS

Spring arrived without asking permission.

The air softened first—the bite of winter traded for something warm and uncertain, carrying the scent of wet earth and honeysuckle. School hallways filled with restless noise, teachers more lenient, windows cracked open to let in sunlight that made even the lockers shine like they'd been forgiven.

Van felt the shift before he could name it. The days no longer dragged; they drifted. Everything was changing again, just quietly enough to pretend it wasn't.

At Heritage Baptist, revival flyers gave way to bright new ones pinned to the bulletin board—"**Camp Cardinal's Nest: Fellowship. Renewal. Purpose.**"

The paper glowed gold under the fluorescent light, the smiling faces of last summer's campers frozen mid-laughter. Pastor Rich had already announced from the pulpit that the youth program would attend as a group. "A week to strengthen bonds in Christ," he'd said, his voice full and certain.

Van's stomach had turned at the thought.

Bonds were already complicated enough.

. . .

THE WEEKS since Colby's sleepover had unfolded in slow, uneasy balance. They still laughed in practice, still traded glances across the field, but something hung between them—unspoken and fragile. When their shoulders brushed, neither pulled away. When Colby's hand lingered a moment too long passing him the ball, the spark was still there, quieter now but undeniable.

And yet, neither spoke of that night.

Sometimes Van caught himself replaying it—the mint, the hush, the warmth—and his chest would tighten, both with memory and with fear of losing it. Other times, he wondered if Colby remembered it at all.

Jeremiah and Daphne, meanwhile, had become so perfectly rehearsed they almost stopped looking real.

At church, they sat front-row center, hands linked just loosely enough to appear holy. In the halls, their laughter rose like a cue line. Pastor Rich beamed each time someone called them a model couple. But Van saw what others missed—the way Jeremiah's smile flickered a split second too late, the weight in his shoulders when Daphne's voice grew too bright.

It wasn't love. It was a performance everyone demanded stay standing.

CHOIR REHEARSALS TURNED toward spring hymns—"Fairest Lord Jesus," "In the Garden," songs meant for soft light and open windows. Mrs. Whitaker's baton still snapped, but even she had softened with the season, humming when she thought no one was listening.

Van sang quietly one afternoon after class, alone in the gym while she packed her things. His voice drifted through the rafters —unrehearsed, unguarded. For once, he didn't try to make it perfect. He just let it be his.

When the final note faded, he looked up and found Mrs.

Whitaker watching him from the doorway. She smiled, faint but real.

"You're finding it," she said. "Whatever it is."

He nodded, unsure what she meant but feeling it anyway.

AT SOCCER PRACTICE, the air shimmered with pollen and heat. Coach Thomas barked less now, his voice tired, the season nearly over. Jeremiah's focus was elsewhere; his passes off, his laughter forced. When Daphne called from the fence, he looked—but not the way he used to.

Colby stayed steady. Always steady.

"Plant," he said quietly as they ran drills side by side. "You'll hold your ground better if you don't look for where the hit's coming from."

Van did. The advice worked. The block was clean, the sting of the ball against his shin grounding him more than any applause.

When practice ended, they walked toward the parking lot together, the low sun bleeding orange across the field. The world smelled like cut grass and rain. For a while, neither spoke. Then Colby nodded toward the church steeple visible in the distance.

"You going to that camp thing?"

Van shrugged. "Don't know. Dad says I probably should."

Colby kicked at a loose pebble, sending it skipping down the asphalt. "Yeah. My mom signed me up already. Says it'll be good for me."

He smirked, though his tone wasn't joking. "Guess we'll both find out what 'good' means."

They stood at the edge of the lot, the hum of insects thick in the air. The quiet between them was full—heavy with everything they hadn't said.

Van wanted to tell him he'd been thinking about that night every day since. That he didn't know what it meant yet, but it meant something. Instead, he said softly, "You think it'll be different there?"

Colby glanced sideways. "Everything's different when adults aren't watching."

Then, with that half-grin that always managed to undo him, he added, "You'll see."

Van's pulse tripped. He didn't know if it was a promise or a warning. Maybe both.

SUNDAY CAME with its usual rhythm—coffee and perfume, pews creaking, sermons about walking in the light. Van sat in the loft, half-listening, his gaze drifting to the sunlight spilling through the stained glass. Dust motes floated like suspended stars, and somewhere below, Jeremiah's voice mingled with Daphne's in the hymn.

Van's hand brushed against the folded camp flyer tucked in his Bible.

The paper was soft from being handled too much, the edges curling slightly. The words "**Strengthen Your Faith. Define Your Future.**" were printed in bold gold letters.

He traced them with his thumb, the ink smudging faintly.

When the final hymn rose through the sanctuary, Van's voice joined it—low, uncertain, but clear. He wasn't sure what he believed anymore, not about faith, not about friendship, not even about himself. But as the sound filled the space around him, he knew one thing:

Something was coming.

Something that would unravel everything he thought he understood—about Jeremiah, about Colby, about the quiet lines that separated who he was from who he was expected to be.

And as the congregation sang "**Amen,**" Van lifted his eyes toward the stained glass window, where sunlight burned through the reds and golds like fire.

He didn't know it yet, but the next chapter of his life—the one that would begin under the high pines and heat of **Camp Cardinal's Nest**—was already waiting, just beyond the edge of spring.

"Every burden teaches us the weight of what we'll carry next."

THE CARDINAL'S CALL

Epilogue – **The Cardinal's Call**

Spring lingered longer than it should have, stretching the days thin with light that refused to fade.

The church lawn grew wild around the edges, azaleas blooming like bruises beneath the stained-glass windows. Every Sunday bled into the next until the hymns blurred together—soft, practiced, unchanging.

At home, everything carried on as if nothing had shifted.

His father's footsteps still echoed down the hallway before dawn.

His mother still hummed while folding laundry.

Emmalee still chased dust motes through sunbeams like they were angels hiding in the light.

But inside Van, something was different.

Quietly. Permanently.

He still caught himself glancing toward the street corner at night, half-expecting the flicker of headlights—the shape of a truck slowing just long enough to be real. It never came. But every time the wind moved the trees, he thought he could still feel it—the pull of that night, the spark that had cracked something open inside him.

Colby's words echoed like a hymn he couldn't forget.

Don't forget that night.

He hadn't.

The memory pulsed under everything—the sermons, the small talk, the pretending. It was alive in his chest, untamed and whispering.

By June, flyers began appearing on the church bulletin board, corners curling from the heat:

CAMP CARDINAL'S NEST BIBLE CAMP

Faith. Fellowship. Renewal.

His mother circled the date before he could even ask.

"It'll be good for you," she said, smoothing the page flat with her hand. "Pastor Rich says the boys' cabin will be full this year. Jeremiah's already signed up."

Van nodded, pretending he hadn't already seen Colby's name scribbled at the bottom of the list.

That night, the air hummed with the kind of stillness that only comes before a storm. Fireflies blinked over the grass, rising one by one until the yard shimmered. He sat on the porch steps, bare feet against the cool concrete, watching the world flicker alive.

He thought of the lake he'd heard about at Camp Cardinal's Nest—the one they said stayed so still it could swallow the stars.

He thought of Colby's voice—low, certain—and the way the world had shifted after.

And for the first time, he wondered if maybe God's voice wasn't in the thunder at all, but in the spaces that came before it.

Somewhere in the distance, a train called out—a long, low wail that sounded like a beginning.

The kind that said something was coming.

The kind that didn't ask permission.

Van didn't know it yet, but the summer waiting beyond those

church doors would demand more of him than silence could ever protect.

He was about to learn what it meant to carry a truth that refused to stay buried.

And when the cardinal finally called, he would have to decide which voice he'd answer.

End of Book One
   Burdens Beneath the Hymns

NEXT IN THE UNBURDENED SERIES:
   Book Two – The Weight of Witness

ABOUT THE AUTHOR

JR Gray-Heim is a North Carolina–based author whose work blends vivid story-telling with raw emotional depth, creating narratives that linger long after the last page. With a background as both a creative visionary and community builder, Gray-Heim writes with a voice that is as intimate as it is universal—capturing the weight of burden, resilience, and redemption in the human spirit.

Beyond writing, Gray-Heim is a salon owner, educator, and philanthropist, dedicated to elevating both art and community. When not immersed in his latest manuscript, he can be found designing intentional spaces, mentoring young artists, or championing local causes.

The Unburdened Series marks Gray-Heim's debut into the literary world—an exploration of the ties that bind us, the secrets that haunt us, and the strength it takes to break free.

ACKNOWLEDGMENTS

To my husband, **Adam** — your love, patience, and unwavering belief in me carried this story when I questioned whether I could. You have been my calm, my compass, and my constant reminder that authenticity is always worth the risk. This book exists because you never stopped believing in what I had to say. And to our son, **Caleb** — your courage, humor, and kindness have shown me what true strength looks like. Watching you grow into yourself has been one of my life's greatest honors. You remind me daily why stories like this matter — because somewhere, someone is still trying to find their way home, too.

To my mentors, teachers, and creative guides — thank you for showing me how to shape chaos into story and emotion into truth. Your insight gave this book structure; your encouragement gave it courage.

To the early readers who saw the heart of *Burdens Beneath the Hymns* long before when it started as *Repentance of the Southern Burden* — your faith in these pages kept me going. You recognized the pulse of this story and pushed me forward when I couldn't see how to take another step.

And finally, to everyone who has ever carried the weight of their own story — this book is for you. The struggles we survive, the love we find, and the truths we learn to speak are not small things. You reminded me that healing doesn't come from perfection, but from being seen.

Thank you — truly — for allowing this story to find you.

— JR Gray-Heim